BOLT ACTION

Harry Lang

Table of Contents

Dedication

To my wife and best friend, Denise, who passed away far too soon.

I miss your smiles when discussing my writing.

Thank you for loving me.

Harry

Acknowledgements

To Paul, who started this journey with me eight years ago and has been at my side ever since.

To Michael, for the many laughs we shared.

To Kirk, who never complains when I discuss my writing.

About the Author

At 88 years young, I can hardly believe I'm still writing! My journey as an author began at the age of 82, proving that it's never too late to pursue a passion. This is my fifth novel, and writing has brought an entirely new dimension to my life in my senior years. It has been a journey of discovery, creativity, and endless joy—one that I never could have imagined but now couldn't live without.

Prologue

It has become appallingly obvious that our technology has exceeded our humanity.

Albert Einstein

0

Return To Darkness

Shaolin Temple

Songshan Mountain

Zhengding, China

January 15, Present year

The early morning sun glided over the rooftops, reflecting on the complete solitude encompassing the monastery. A small two-lane road ran close to the fields of produce used to feed the many monks and local citizens dependent on the monastery for food. Adjacent to the fields were pens for the highly prized pork products favored by the local citizens.

A clear section of land was marked off by stakes with different colored ribbons, noting the importance of the martial arts training area in the complex.

Two elderly Buddhist monks, Brother Zheng and Brother Lee, walked carefully around the martial arts area, both deep in thought.

Brother Lee broke the silence, turning to Brother Zheng. "You have spent a great deal of time with new Brother Ram. It appears you know him?"

"Yes," Zheng replied solemnly. "It is most unfortunate to meet with him once more. In the past, he was a young man attempting to free himself of demons. He confided in me that his name was Hull. He had suffered betrayal resulting in the death of his wife and infant daughter. His arrival ended a very dark period in his life. As before, he walked thirty kilometers from the airport, appearing at our front gate. In the past, we succeeded—after many stressful months—in helping him free his mind of past events. I am not certain he can ever be freed of the demons which control him," Brother Zheng spoke painfully.

"You had to move him away from the others, as his shouting and actions were keeping the other brothers awake. Brother Ram appears not to sleep. He has been extremely helpful in leading the Kung Fu training every morning. His skills have not gone unnoticed by the others—especially the Chinese Major Li Hue, who enters our grounds without impunity."

"Yes, I have observed how he treats Brother Ram," Zheng replied, his voice strained. "The Chinese major waits until Ram is working in the fields before harassing him—calling him 'his pet pig' while striking him with his riding crop, leaving welts on Ram's body. True to our code of nonviolence, Ram just takes the punishment without striking back. Ram has confided in me, telling me he understands China rules the temple and surrounding areas. Striking the major would bring vengeance and hardship to the temple. I am fearful Ram could lose himself."

1

Sudden death

Vladivostok Russia

2100 Hours

The scent of the sea permeated the entire city. A mixture of oil, gasoline, and fish was a pleasant reminder to Yale "Rusty" Rutstein of why he had decided to live and raise a family in a village close to this large port city. He laughed at his young son following him, playing with their two large dogs. The laugh was more ironic, as "Rusty" Rutstein was a mail carrier who had many dangerous encounters with dogs during his working days. He called to his son to follow him, with the two dogs trailing his every step. He looked skyward as a blue light descended on the group.

Rusty's supervisor, Petr Kaskov, remarked to his driver, "Rusty has never been late or absent from work in all the time I've known him. I bet too much vodka has his head spinning."

Ringing the doorbell to gain the attention of anyone living in the house, they were surprised to find the front door slightly ajar, opening further when Petr touched it by accident. The two men shouted once inside the house, both freezing as they heard a sob and a low moan coming from the kitchen.

There, a sobbing woman sat with her head resting on the kitchen table. Petr placed a hand on the woman's shoulder—partly to comfort her and partly to let her know they were present. Finally, her tear-filled eyes opened to gaze at the two men. Still sobbing, she pointed toward the backyard and then placed her head back on the table, wailing in her grief.

Petr and his companion opened the door to the grassy, wet backyard. Peering through the mist, they spotted the outline of a large dog lying on the grass. Not knowing what to expect, both men tread carefully toward the stationary body, only to trip over the dead body of Rusty.

In disbelief, the two men saw that Rusty's mouth and eyes were open. Standing erect nearby were the bodies of Rusty's son and second dog—both with eyes and mouths open.

Retreating to the house, Petr took out his cell phone and, in a raspy, emotion-filled voice, dialed the local military authorities.

***

Hongcum Administrative Village

Huang Mountains, China

0500 Hours

Li Feng was a young, ambitious man. He and his wife had just finished their morning tea. It was time to tend to their small but growing flock of sheep. The COVID plague had stopped all meat production for several months in their area. Now, the government was offering incentives in the form of currency, living accommodations, and even an automobile for the largest increase in production, as decided by the local political administrator.

Li knew he had no chance at any large prize, but he and his young wife had planned to grow their flock for the children they hoped to have. Living remotely from the main village was a blessing to them. Their lead sheepdog loved being fed by the couple and came running to greet them. As he approached, Li's wife raised her hand to shield her face. A bolt of blue came from nowhere.

Hi Feng was angry at his young neighbors. He had used the phone three times to contact them. Thinking they were ignoring him because of his advanced age, he rode his bike over to their small farm to complain about their sheep grazing on his land.

Li Feng had very little contact with his neighbors—only polite greetings at the community marketplace. Still, he was becoming more irritated by the moment as he called for one or both of them to come out. Walking carefully on the wet and slippery ground, he wiped his glasses and noticed a mound in the field—unusual for this flat farmland.

His first thought was that the lazy young couple was sleeping in the middle of the day. But when he saw the two of them lying with their mouths and eyes wide open, he realized they were not alive.

His first action was to walk quickly back to his bike, pedal home, and contact the village council's law officer.

***

Slidell, Louisiana

0400 Hours

Fishing Ramp

Jeff "Whitey" Kemp was a very happy man. He was approaching his truck, ready to pull in his best catch of shrimp for the season. Prices were high, and the seafood distributor had a good-looking daughter. Hitting the entrance fob on his remote, he climbed into his truck, which was already attached to a trailer.

Backing up slowly, he stopped the truck with the rear wheels half in the water. Attaching his boat to the trailer, he began to pull the boat from the water—stopping only when a blue light struck the front of his truck.

Paul Sast turned to his brother Tom. "Can't put our boat in until the dumbass with his boat and truck blocking the way moves. Hey mister, do you mind pulling your boat out of the water? Real fishermen would like a chance."

"I don't think he heard you," Tom shouted. "Let me go down there and make our point—with my fist if necessary."

Tom shuffled in his waders toward the truck, which was still idling. The window was open, but what he saw made him rub his eyes again to make sure his vision wasn't playing tricks on him.

"Call the sheriff and then come down here. Your eyes have to see this," Tom called to his brother.

Puzzled, Paul called the local sheriff's office as directed, then walked quickly toward the truck. Tom's eyes were glassy, his face contorted in disbelief.

"Take a look at the man's face and eyes," Tom told Paul. "Both his mouth and eyes are open—but he's dead."

***

A month later, the same scenario appeared in different locations across each country. Stariysa, on the Volga River in Russia; Tongli, a small town by the water in China; and Ashland, Wisconsin, in the upper Midwest of the United States.

Two months after the initial mysterious events, the small town of Kirillov—home to one of the world's largest monasteries in Russia—became the scene of another strange case. So did Suzhou in China. And who could explain what happened to an entire family living on the outskirts of Lawton, Oklahoma, in the United States?

Law enforcement, medical professionals, and government officials in all three countries were befuddled by the strange death scenes: humans and animals alike, all with mouths and eyes wide open, yet clearly no longer breathing.

The press in each country was kept in the dark to prevent spreading panic among the general public.

2

Beginning of Danger

Bremen Germany

December 31, 1944

Unterseeboot U-331

A light scattering of snow fell on one of the Kriegsmarine's newest Type XXI submarines. Newly fitted with the most advanced snorkel innovation, it allowed the vessel to avoid surfacing for battery recharging. Vice-Admiral Kent Belanger addressed the young man standing beside him on the officer's deck.

"Herr Ernst, be prepared to have your family board my vessel with the other scientists and their families in thirty minutes. Herr Braum, the rocket scientist; Herr Hickler, the leader of the Einsatzgruppen death squads; and Herr Haver, the electronics expert, will join you on this journey. All of you are young and carry our fight of *Wolfhold* into the future.

"I was told—rather, instructed—to meet with you alone. The substances you are taking with you are very lethal, I understand. My question to you, since we are alone, is this: why are you so special in the Nazi hierarchy that you were given space on my vessel, while others must use more dangerous ratlines and sympathetic religious sites to travel far riskier routes to safety in South America? I am even more curious, as you are completely unknown to myself or any of my crew."

Rudi Ernst smiled at Belanger. "Do not be alarmed, Vice-Admiral; I have taken every precaution to safeguard everyone traveling with us to Argentinien. It is enclosed in a leak-proof glass bottle placed inside a solid lead container. It will stay in my possession for the entire journey.

"To better answer your question about why I was selected by your superiors to travel with you, I must ask you a question. Do you have any knowledge of the camps we send Juden and other undesirables to?" Rudolph "Rudi" Ernst spoke slowly so as not to be misunderstood.

"Sadly, I do not know much about the camps, other than that they house people considered dangerous to the Reich. But that still doesn't explain why you were awarded space to a secure location." Belanger was becoming perturbed with the young man.

"The people in these camps have become a problem for the German high command. Along with others, I was tasked with finding a *final solution* for the increasing numbers. My formulas were used to create a special form of Zyklon gas used to dispose of inmates deemed most worthy of killing.

"I was working on a new, improved formula—supervised by *Wolfhold's* high command—which would work in open spaces. My work requires more time to prove effective. That is the main reason I was given preferential treatment: to bring my new design to the battlefield, now or in the future.

"You can only imagine what would happen to me if the Americans or Russians were to capture me." Ernst noticed Belanger's face grow drawn and pale at his words.

"Go join your family. I will be speaking with you and the other scientists in a few minutes," Vice-Admiral Belanger said, shaking Ernst's hand.

"This is a very different type of combat mission," Ludwig Onst, second-in-command, mused to the Vice-Admiral.

"Ludwig, I can be honest with you. Admiral Canaris—our superior and a brilliant officer—confided in me over lunch last week. We were given this elite mission only because Germany's final hope of victory ended in the forests of the Ardennes last week.

"I was told the young scientists and their families are the lifeblood of the future Fourth Reich. We can carry only half our supply of munitions. Our mission is to make certain these highly important, skilled citizens are delivered safely to the small port of Bahia Blanca. There, they will meet German families already settled in Fürth, Argentina—a secret scientific community known only to a select few.

"Canaris told me the Führer himself has diverted precious resources to this vital war effort. He has even given us additional protection, since our mission is so critical. Like the U-140, we have special rubber panels attached to the sides of our vessel. These panels make us invisible to enemy radar, which has detected and destroyed many of our comrades. These innovations prove how vital our mission has become.

"In addition, gold from the Merkers salt mines has been stored aboard. Our instructions are to use our weapons only to defend ourselves. You noticed the U-864 on the next loading platform, also preparing for a lengthy voyage. Their leader, more of a political appointee than an experienced seaman, said their cargo consists of a rare element that would assist the Japanese in building a weapon to defeat our common enemies."

Vice-Admiral Belanger gave Ludwig permission to leave, having fully explained the dangers of their voyage.

***

"What did the commander of the submarine discuss with you, Rudi?" Heidi Ernst searched her husband's eyes for any information he had learned.

"Nothing, other than he will speak to all of our companions in a few minutes. He understands my package is safe with the safeguards I've taken, but he requested that I keep it in my possession at all times." Ernst held Heidi's face to dispel any doubts she might have—though he himself had reservations about their method of transportation.

***

"Please stand under the shelter my crew has erected to shield you from the rain," Vice-Admiral Belanger said, standing on the deck of his submarine, which rose several meters above the assembled gathering of young men, women, and children below.

"My name is Belanger. I am the commander of this vessel, which will transport you to Bahia Blanca. This is a ship of war that has been altered to accommodate your luggage and instruments. But I must caution all of you: although we have charted a course far removed from areas of military importance, there is a chance our enemies may have listening devices on ships or other vessels in our path.

"The light in your living quarters will turn blue, warning all that no sounds should be made. I see a number of very small children who, I am sure, will not understand complete silence. Maintaining absolute silence is critical to our success. Parents, I must have your complete cooperation to ensure this happens.

"Now, your boarding will be directed by members of my crew. Follow them to your living quarters, which are sparse but livable. I will visit your quarters from time to time to update you on our progress.

"One last thing: we will depart in three hours. The night sky is dark, giving us protection from enemy attacks. Most of our travel will be accomplished underwater due to a new breathing apparatus we have installed. Good night for now—adapt quickly to your new living quarters."

Commander Belanger thought to himself, *We will need a miracle if we are detected.*

3

Alert the President

Oval Office White House

0700 Hours

March 28

President Bradley Beatherd sat at his desk, reading briefs from his staff detailing trouble spots in the country and around the world. Sitting alone with his specially brewed coffee afforded him time to think and reflect on the myriad problems confronting him on a daily basis.

He mused to himself, *This is the best time of day for me—no tie, great coffee,* and, thanks to direct orders to his staff, *no calls or personal interruptions unless there's a national emergency.* He had emphasized those stringent rules during the first week of his presidency to his chief of staff, John Ashley, who served as his gatekeeper.

Glancing at his watch, he noted that the daily rush would begin at 0900 hours, meaning he still had plenty of time to finish his coffee and put on a tie around his thick, muscular neck—developed through constant physical conditioning, including weightlifting sessions with members of his security detail.

Beatherd was stunned when his chief of staff came racing through the door.

"Sorry, Mr. President, we have a DEFCON emergency. I need your security detail to escort you to the PEOC—Presidential Emergency Operations Center—immediately. A situation has developed with the Chinese and Russians that demands your immediate involvement."

Ashley's face—normally smiling and cheerful—was pale, drawn, and definitely not smiling. Beatherd also noticed Ashley was carrying his revolver.

The President walked briskly, surrounded by his security detail, who—he observed—had their weapons drawn and carried at their sides, which was definitely not standard procedure.

His curiosity deepened when he saw military personnel standing in the hallway with automatic weapons, guarding the White House corridors—an extremely rare sight.

He was transported back in memory to his first mission as a lieutenant in the Rangers. *Adrenaline mixed with the unknown will quicken your heart rate every time,* he thought.

The lead security agent knocked twice at the door, signaling the agent on the inside to open it.

Ashley moved into the room, leading the President. Beatherd nearly fell to his knees at the scene that greeted him.

Secretary of State Bluthe was in running attire, dripping with sweat, which was being soaked up by the two towels draped around his neck.

The Secretary of Homeland Security, Patricia Hevier—normally dressed in expensive suits or highly tailored pantsuits—was wearing Bermuda shorts, loafers, and a bandana covering her blonde hair.

The Chairman of the Joint Chiefs of Staff, General Patrick Heaton, stood in full battle fatigues, a revolver hugging his left hip.

Plasma screens filled every corner of the room, dominated by a life-size projection centered on the front wall.

Beatherd took another breath and thought to himself, *What in the hell is going on?*

4

Arrival in Bahia Blanca

January 7, 1945

Bahia Blanco, Argentine

1300 Hours

Rudi Ernst's knees buckled as he carefully stepped down the metal stairs leading from the submarine. He turned to assist his two children and then his wife, who now stood on firm ground—a completely different feeling from the constant motion aboard the submarine.

His family was quickly surrounded by a welcoming party of Germans who had arrived in Bahía Blanca on earlier missions. Rudi was met by two young men who offered to carry his container.

"Nein," Rudi answered, clutching the container even more tightly. "Show me the transportation to the laboratory."

The two young men directed him to a large truck, where all the luggage from the new arrivals was being loaded by other helping hands. Satisfied, Rudi climbed into the passenger seat, still guarding the canister with a vise-like grip.

His wife sat next to him as they rode toward their new home.

"Our children are as tired as I am," she said softly. "No unpacking today—just a chance to sleep in a decent bed, my husband."

"Yes. They behaved better than I had hoped," Rudi replied. "The scare when the commander thought we had been recognized by the enemy was the most alarming moment. Yet not a sound came from them. The crew appreciated our conduct. The adults were given beer, and the children, special cakes."

He glanced down at the container in his lap. "Like you, I am very tired. But I must store this container in a safe, guarded environment. Without the proper safeguards, the contents would bring a slow, painful death. I will join you after I've secured it at the laboratory. I won't feel bad if you and the children are asleep when I return."

Rudi knew he was operating on adrenaline alone, fully aware of what his superiors expected from him.

The truck dropped off Rudi's wife, son, and daughter at the small home that had been constructed the previous month in anticipation of their arrival. After kissing his family goodbye, Rudi remained aboard the truck, which continued for another fifteen minutes before stopping in front of his new laboratory—aptly named *Science 1*—with a spotlight illuminating the name.

He had been told the keys would be in the door. Ascending four pale green-painted steps, he turned the key and entered what would be his workplace for the foreseeable future. One light had been left on for him, and he quickly scanned the room for the switch.

Flipping on the rest of the lights, Rudi was impressed. The size and quality of the equipment surpassed his expectations.

Suddenly, the door creaked open. A blinding flashlight beamed directly into Rudi's eyes, leaving him unable to see the figure stepping into the room.

"Please keep your hands where I can see them," the voice ordered. "My name is Richard Hickler. I am head of security for this complex. This laboratory is only to be used by the lead scientist sent from the Fatherland. I was alarmed when I saw a light in the window. Do you have the proper credentials to be here, or are you trespassing? Show me your papers, please, or I will be forced to shoot you—no questions asked."

Rudi's heart pounded. He knew who Hickler was—the feared head of the *Einsatzgruppen*, the paramilitary "death squads" created to eliminate men, women, and children in conquered territories.

With trembling hands, Rudi held out his papers for inspection.

Hickler scanned the documents. "Sorry for the inconvenience, Herr Ernst," he said, lowering the flashlight. "One cannot be too careful. Before you use the laboratory, please call the number on the card I'm giving you."

He handed over a small card, then turned sharply on his heel—his boots clicking on the floor—and exited, leaving Rudi standing with the card still in his outstretched hand.

Rudi found a desk and chair and slowly opened the leather pouch that had been given to him by Himmler himself. His head throbbed from lack of sleep, and his eyes burned.

Heinrich Himmler, second only to Adolf Hitler in the Nazi regime, had met with Rudi briefly in Berlin. The meeting had been short and to the point: Himmler had handed him the brown pouch, marked with the Reichsführer's initials etched into the fine leather.

Withdrawing the letter on Hitler's stationery, Rudi read:

Herr Ernst,

You and the other young scientists are the future of the Fourth Reich. Funding for you and the others is secure for the next twenty years. If more money is needed, contact the group supervisor. He will have methods known only to him for securing additional funds for your projects.

Heil Hitler

The phrase was scrawled hastily at the bottom.

Rudi reviewed the letter one more time before returning it to the pouch. He turned off all the lights except one, locked the door, slipped the key and the card into his jacket pocket, and returned to the truck waiting outside.

5

Hull Identified

PEOC

January 31

White House

President Beatherd had survived many firefights during his time in the military. Nothing compared to seeing the withdrawn and worried expressions on the faces of his cabinet officers. More concerning was the military personnel standing with their weapons in a ready-to-fire position.

Secretary of Defense Sheldon Bluthe, sweat still evident on the towel wrapped around his face and neck, stepped forward and positioned himself beside Beatherd.

"Mr. President, both China and Russia are issuing orders to their armed forces to defend their countries. Apparently, they have been subject to unknown deadly attacks and are blaming us for the deaths of several of their citizens over a three-month period."

Patricia Hevier, Secretary of Homeland Security, replaced Bluthe at the President's side.

"Mr. President, I replied to the Chinese and Russian governments that we in the United States have also been subject to the same type of unknown attacks on our citizens. Both countries agreed to slow down their military posture if I could provide visual proof. Fortunately, I had pictures sent to me by concerned law enforcement and medical personnel that I could share with them. Both remarked that the cause of death was strange—nothing they had ever seen.

"China and Russia are now alerting their special forces to prepare personnel equipped to handle this situation. From our discussions, we put together a checklist of the qualities needed in an individual to combat this unknown terror. We've written these qualities on the whiteboard, with the understanding that we will confer again before they take any further military action. I broached the subject of a joint operation with them. I'm not fluent in Russian or Chinese, but I believe their response was something like, 'Over our dead bodies' would they allow any American into a joint operation."

Directing his attention to the whiteboard, Kenneth James, former head of the CIA, spoke directly to Beatherd.

"You can read while I speak. We have a situation before us with no precedent. Humans in different countries are dying of suffocation—in broad daylight, in open surroundings. There's no visible cause of death, no knowledge of who is causing these horrific deaths, or where the attack is coming from. We brainstormed the qualities needed in a person to lead a mission with these many unknowns."

James took a sip from his water glass and continued.

"Obviously, the person must possess extraordinary intelligence, physical skill—since we don't know what types of violence may be faced—fluency in several languages, again because we don't know the enemy's location. They must understand current and future technology, ideally have some knowledge of business for potential negotiations, and lastly, be familiar with weapons. We simply don't know what types or numbers of dangers will be encountered."

James sat down, visibly upset.

The room became silent. Finally, Beatherd stood up.

"Great work on short notice. To summarize, we need a Superman with superior negotiating skills, who can speak multiple languages and understand complex technical or scientific research."

Beatherd smiled grimly, turned to the whiteboard, then sat back down.

Secretary of Defense Bluthe rose again to address the President.

"I contacted my counterparts in Russia and China, sharing our concern regarding potential hostilities. I relayed the list of attributes we're looking for in someone to lead a multinational team. As you can imagine, they concurred—they had compiled a similar list.

"A fleeting moment later, the head of China's PLA—their version of our Navy SEALs—rejoined the conversation. He spoke one word I didn't understand: 'Hull.' He said it again, louder this time, seeing that I didn't recognize it. 'You have a soldier named Hull. We admired his tactical and combat skills when he was part of our special forces.' I wrote the name down on my notepad. Then the head of Russia's Spetsnaz returned to the meeting. He had a big grin on his face. His words were, 'Hull is fine with us. Just mention to him I want a rematch in our vodka drinking contest.'

"I questioned him again to make sure I heard correctly. He confirmed: 'Hull is acceptable to us.' The leaders of the Russian and Chinese special military units agreed—Hull would be the perfect person to lead a multinational security force."

He watched the screen go blank, then turned toward the President.

President Beatherd stood up.

"I can't say I'm overjoyed with China and Russia telling us we have the person to lead a combat operation, but if it solves our problem—go contact Hull."

Beatherd left no doubt in his tone that he wanted action yesterday.

Before he had a chance to reach the door, Secretary of Defense Daniel Beard stood up and addressed the room.

"We have a problem. A big problem. We cannot locate or find Hull after August of last year. We know he was in Lawton, Oklahoma, on the tenth. After that, he vanished."

The President spoke slowly and loudly so all parties understood.

"Find him—or I will have new Secretaries by next week."

Ashley escorted the President out the door.

6

Paris Meeting

March 1

Bouillon Chartier

Paris

1230 Hours

Viktor Novak, President and CEO of Trotsky Armaments, was the first to arrive. He gave the hostess his name for the reservation he had made last month. The hostess gave him her most welcoming smile and escorted him to the remote table he had requested. He was pleased to see that his favorite cocktail was already waiting for him.

He smiled inwardly. Max Parris, owner of Alpha Dynamics in the United States, must have tipped an exorbitant amount the last time the three of them had met with the German scientists. This restaurant was known for its world-class cuisine and its refined, expensive ornaments of dining pleasure. He looked at the bourgeoisie paintings and sculptures adorning the walls. Strange, he thought, lighting up his perpetual Russian cigarette, how Bao Ming, a relative of the current Chinese Premier, had at first been doubtful of the new German technology.

It was only after the events that had occurred worldwide in the last two months that Bao requested a meeting of the three. It was standard practice that when the military leaders of the three nations came together, every leading military defense-related organization would follow. No company wanted to miss the opportunity for substantial weapons systems that required funding for development. Max had considered how limited civilian casualties—planned for maximum effectiveness—could and would result in huge profits for the three of them. Max Parris had, indeed, created a worldwide uneasiness controlled by their alliance.

Parris walked in with Ming at his side.

"Sorry," Ming said in perfect English. "Paris traffic becomes worse every year. Soon it will rival what the traffic in Beijing is like." He laughed at his reference to the chaotic driving problems that existed in the center of power for his country.

Parris spoke. "First, thank you for speaking in English. Foreign languages are not a priority in our educational system. I'm trying to learn French so the three of us can converse in a shared verbal environment. We agreed the German's description of his new weapon technology four months ago sounded like the ravings of a maniac. Yet, we funded a trial period—but not before we opened new facilities devoted entirely to dangers from space and unknown sources. No other organization in my country had resources dedicated to the strange deaths occurring. I take it the same situation has developed in your countries?"

Both Ming and Novak signaled their agreement.

"Being both unknown and lethal, my government cannot channel monies into my organization fast enough," Novak said. Outspoken as always, he could hardly mask his excitement at his good fortune.

Bao Ming, the most reserved in speech, said in a very soft voice, "The experiment has been a huge success for me and my organization." He looked at his companions. "The experiments must continue, and we must pay the German scientists what they requested to prepare future strikes under our guidance. We all must initiate a defense should any person or organization attempt to find and stop our golden goose."

Parris commented, "I am way ahead of you. Yesterday, I hired ten men and women who are in positions to infiltrate any government agencies to ensure we always stay one step ahead of our competition—and our governments. They can use their day jobs to add to our knowledge and security. Speaking with the Germans, I learned they have trained a special military team to eliminate any threats we perceive. I personally spoke to their leader, Kim Hickler—a most imposing young lady.

"In addition, I have new smartwatches for each of you. I call them *Genius*. My background in high-level computing technology makes them the perfect communication tool for us. It will serve as our link to one another in your native languages. *Genius* has the programming power to take your words and make them understood by the other two. Your watch uses 256-bit encryption. Any message sent or received will be unintelligible until you press the Alt and dollar sign keys. The message will then appear in your native language. I designed the communication system to link to a central message center to keep all of us informed in real time about what's happening with our shared financial goals. All alerts will be both visual and audio."

Novak raised his glass to his companions. "To our success, gentlemen."

As they were raising their glasses in a much-deserved toast, the in-house photographer walked by.

"You gentlemen need a picture to keep as a remembrance." She snapped three photos. Turning to Novak, she said, "I have your email address from your last visit. I'll send them to you to share with your friends."

Novak could only grin. "Those pictures will cost me a thousand euros, but they'll serve as a splendid reminder of our audacious plot—one that will add massive amounts to all of our fortunes."

7

White House Hull Located

White House

President's Study

March 7 0700 Hours

John Ashley wondered out loud who his next employer might be as he gently but firmly knocked on the door to the President's secret hiding place—where coffee was consumed while intelligence briefings from various secretaries were highlighted for discussion.

"Come in," Beatherd's unmistakable gruff voice replied to Ashley's knock. "What's so important that you have to disturb my daily torture on the treadmill?"

Large beads of perspiration glistened on his forehead, attesting to the severity of his workout. He grabbed one of the presidential towels, the words *Hail to the Chief* emblazoned on the now-wet fabric.

"Mr. President, we've located Roy G. Hull," Ashley nearly shouted the good news.

"Excellent! Don't tell me the Chinese found him. No—tell me how soon I can speak with him?" Beatherd's breathing was returning to normal. He was clearly excited. Finding a possible solution to the sudden outbreak of global terror had been straining governments worldwide.

"Mr. President, that's the problem." Ashley hesitated, uncertain of how best to phrase the answer. "We checked with Hull's wife, parents, daughter, and close friends. None of them could think of a place where Hull might be. Actually, Hull found himself. In a psychological profile from 2019, he mentioned a Shaolin Buddhist monastery.

We had our Chinese assets verify the information, and it turns out Hull is currently living as a monk at *the* Shaolin Monastery—which, unfortunately, is located in Tibet. As you know, Tibet is controlled by China.

We informed our Chinese embassy that a close military friend of yours had passed away while staying at the monastery. The monastery welcomes people seeking more knowledge about their religion. Secretary Blueth has requested that we be allowed to send a small team of our military personnel to land at a nearby airfield. The plan is to use a small, rented vehicle to transport Hull from the monastery to the airfield. From there, the party and Mr. Hull will be flown back to the United States.

This plan has been approved—pending a phone call from you to the Premier, requesting their assistance."

"How much must I scrape and bow to bring Hull home?" Beatherd asked, without a hint of a smile.

"Plenty," Ashley replied. "You might add that you're sending your friends a prized gift to help bring your friend Hull home."

He paused, then added, "As a gesture of your appreciation, we're sending the Premier one of our prized pigs—for his dining pleasure."

Ashley wasn't smiling either.

8

Buddhist Temple Punishment

Shaolin Monastery

March 8

0530 Hours

The sun was rising as the wind picked up during the last hour, swirling the robes of the elderly monks into uniform, circular patterns.

"If memory serves me, this is the day the Chinese major always makes an appearance without his soldiers," Brother Lee spoke quietly to his companion, Brother Zheng.

"Yes, the absence of his troops always provides the major with no reins on his brutality. I fear Brother Ran will receive more than the usual amount of lashing and degradation today. We can only hope his foundation in our belief of nonviolence will hold strong. I fear it will be fully tested this day," Brother Zheng replied with a regretful breath.

As the two monks continued their journey through the monastery grounds, Major Li Hue's military vehicle came to a sudden stop directly in front of them. Li Hue stepped briskly out of the car, his ever-present riding crop tucked under his arm.

Speaking to Brother Zheng, he smiled cruelly. "Is my pet pig working in the pig pen this morning? I brought a new riding crop with me—this one has metal rivets in the braids. It will ensure that my pet pig breaks his vow of silence when I beat him today.

It continues to trouble me that my previous punishments—even when I shoved his face into the mud—never got a reaction from Brother Ran. Today will be different. I plan to make him beg me to stop."

Major Li Hue appeared fully satisfied with his description of the torment Brother Ran would endure—especially since all the monks were to be ordered to watch.

He scanned the grounds and quickly spotted Brother Ran, who was always the tallest among them. "I see my pet pig now," he said, his eyes narrowing. "From here, you can witness what my punishment does to both his skin and his spirit."

Overcome with excitement, Li Hue bolted from the car, shouting curses as he ran to greet Brother Ran.

9

Buddhists Temple Freedom

Shaolin Monastery

March 8

0700 hours

Colonel Michael "MadMan" Diana was the first person out of the rented hearse. He was soon joined by Daniel Chasey, a retired Master Sergeant and Roy Hull's bodyguard in years past. The hearse had stopped behind a Chinese military vehicle. Diana noticed two elderly monks nearby, engrossed in some activity.

"How's your Chinese?" Diana asked with a smile.

"A great deal better than yours," Chasey replied, grinning. "Hull and I spent months training with the PLA Special Forces back when the nations were more friendly." Stepping forward, Chasey addressed the monks. "My name is Daniel."

To his surprise, the two monks grinned. "Your Chinese is admirable," said Brother Lee, "but we both speak English, which is what the other man used to speak to you. Why are you here, and what is the reason for the vehicle you came in?"

Relieved that speaking Chinese wouldn't be necessary, Diana responded, "We're here for a friend we believe has been studying and meditating in your monastery. He's crucial to resolving a serious situation that has developed in our country. Our objective is to return him home."

The vehicle also held six heavily armed Special Forces soldiers. Diana motioned for them to join him.

Brother Zheng eyed the soldiers before turning back to Diana and Chasey. "There is no need for violence. Our beliefs are rooted in nonviolence, even when attacked. If the person you seek desires to leave the monastery, he is free to do so at any time. I believe the man you are looking for is the one currently being tormented in our pig area."

All eyes turned to witness a disturbing scene: a smaller man delivering blows to a much taller man while shouting, "I will make you beg for mercy," and forcing the man's face into pig slop and mud. The lashings sent waves of pain through Brother Ran—Roy Hull's body.

These beatings never bothered me before, Hull thought painfully. *Am I getting weaker with age?* Mud was caked in his mouth and nose, making breathing difficult.

Diana turned to Chasey. "Do you want to go in and stop the brutality, or should I?"

Chasey smiled and pursed his lips, mimicking the sound of a Montana eagle about to kill its prey.

Hull, covered in mud, stood as the major paused to catch his breath. The sound came again—unmistakable to Hull's ears.

"Let Hull end the beatings in his own special way," Chasey said.

Through mud-caked eyes, Hull could now see his two old friends—Diana and Chasey—standing beside Brothers Zheng and Lee. For a brief moment, his mind hesitated. He wasn't fully clear of the past terrors.

Why are those two here? He wondered.

His second thought: *End the pain.* The Montana eagle's call meant only one thing—Chasey's unique warning during dangerous missions: *"Time to get the hell outta Dodge."*

As the major's arm descended for another strike, Hull's right hand shot up and caught the riding crop mid-air. Startled, the major opened his mouth to shout a command, but Hull grabbed his throat with a vice-like grip.

Before the major could react, Hull snatched the riding crop from his hand, forced his mouth open wider, and jammed the weapon down his throat with such force that only the top of the crop remained visible. Hull delivered a brutal kick to the major's groin, pivoted, and twisted the man's neck until the major was facing backwards. He then slammed him to the ground and wiped the mud from his eyes using the sleeve of the major's uniform.

"Hot damn, did you see that strike?" one of the security personnel shouted. "Those moves were snake-like!"

Another voice echoed, half-laughing, "Did my eyes deceive me, or did he actually shove the riding crop down his throat?"

MadMan Diana grinned. "You haven't seen anything yet. For your information, his name is Hull. He's got snake blood running through his veins."

Hull, his head lowered, approached the elderly monks. "I'm sorry for not practicing the nonviolence you taught me. I mean no disrespect, but I believe there are limits to those beliefs."

Brother Zheng nodded solemnly. "Brother Ran, you have displayed much patience under the major's cruelty. Go now, with your friends."

MadMan turned to Chasey. "You guide Hull to our transport. I'll handle the major's vehicle. I'll make sure it's destroyed by fire before we leave."

Chasey took Hull by the arm. "We promised the funeral home the hearse would be back by 1000 hours. The funeral director has to certify your death—Chinese law, to prevent undesirables from leaving the country. We've got a body bag ready for you to slip into. MadMan has a drug to slow your heart rate for inspection."

He glanced at Hull and smirked. "Given how you look and smell, I doubt the exam will be too thorough."

Hull, still encased in mud, held up a hand. "No drugs. I can lower my heart rate and pulse to catatonic levels. Snake blood, remember? But seriously—when can I shower? I can't even stand myself."

Chasey grinned at his old friend. "No time for niceties. You're scheduled to see the President in twenty hours, and we're already behind. Crawl into that body bag and start playing dead. Between your mud-caked body and that odor, the autopsy should take less than five minutes."

10

White House Rose Garden

White House

Rose Garden

March 9, 0800 hours

The north section of the Rose Garden is the most difficult to view from street level. Today, it was shielded from sight by three large lawn maintenance machines parked in a semicircle— by design. Nine men wearing the uniform of the Public Maintenance Division stood in two rows. The back six stood shoulder to shoulder, preventing even a slight glimpse of the three men positioned in front of them.

The day carried a slight chill, but the sun was beginning to break through, warming the Rose Garden.

John Ashley knocked on the President's door, waiting for the usual, "Come in at your peril." Hearing the expected response, Ashley entered and informed the President of a minor adjustment to the day's schedule.

"Sir, I've arranged an early morning photo shoot for the home-state voters in the Rose Garden. Let me help you with your suit coat. It's a bit chilly, but I think you'll find the walk invigorating before the rest of your schedule wears on you."

President Beatherd never refused an opportunity for fresh air. Walking beside Ashley, he asked, "Any news on locating this man, Hull? It's been almost a week, and the Chinese and Russians are clamoring for action. The good news is that nothing similar to those horrific deaths has happened again this month."

Beatherd stopped suddenly. He coughed more than once, his nostrils flared, and his eyes began to burn.

"What in God's name is that smell?"

Ashley took his arm and guided him to the center of the circle. Eight of the nine men stood at attention. The remaining individual was attempting to wipe mud from his eyes to properly see the people in front of him.

Ashley spoke directly to the President. "Mr. President, the man standing before you is Roy G. Hull. We located him from a print in his study when we interviewed his wife, Tamara. She had no knowledge of when or why her husband had a print of a Buddhist monastery located in Tibet. We engaged a CIA agent in the area to investigate. Her report came back positive. That is why I advised you to contact the Chinese Premier for permission to bring your friend's body home."

"I recognize the smell now," Beatherd laughed. "Growing up raising pigs should have prepared me for the odor—although I never had it caked on my clothes and body. Why are Hull's hands and feet shackled like a common criminal?"

"Sir," said Colonel Randy Bell, stepping forward, "not more than twenty-four hours ago, we saw this man use his skills to kill a Chinese major with a ferocity and speed that my words cannot adequately describe. On my orders, we shackled him to ensure history would not repeat itself during this meeting."

Beatherd stepped closer to Hull. "Son, is that right? Did you kill a Chinese officer?" He then turned to the Secret Service agent at his side. "Chamber a round for me and hand me your sidearm. I need to ask this young man named Hull some questions face-to-face."

Taking the revolver in his right hand, Beatherd stepped directly in front of Hull.

"Just so you know, I've seen combat, and I assure you, I know how to use this weapon."

He noticed the six Special Forces men with their revolvers resting easily at their sides—none trusting the President's ability to stop Hull if necessary.

"Just one question. Mr. Hull, why did the major need killing?"

Beatherd stood, waiting for a reply.

Hull adjusted his gaze, trying to clear his vision. The mud had caked his eyelids, making it difficult to see even at short distances.

"Sir, I can answer your question if you'll allow one of my friends to lift my shirt. I can't do it myself."

Beatherd nodded, permitting Chasey to raise Hull's work clothes over his head. Hull turned his back to the President, Ashley, and the Secret Service personnel.

Whip lashes—some healed, some beginning to heal, and some still bleeding—made a lasting impression on Beatherd and Ashley.

Beatherd issued a sharp command. "Unshackle this man immediately. Damn good reason for killing the man who inflicted those wounds on you."

He turned to Ashley. "John, I want this man cleaned up, wounds treated, and ready to be my guest at 1900 hours in my private dining quarters."

Without another word, Beatherd turned and strode quickly back toward the White House.

***

Office of Allen Parris

Alpha Dynamics

1200 Hours

Parris keyed into his "genius" smartphone:

Have scheduled another test with our German friends within the next seven days. Asked that they select larger targets in each country to give some urgency to our solutions.

He hit send—ensuring only his companions would receive and understand the message.

11

Hull Dines with President

White House

Presidential Dining area

1900 Hours

Hull was escorted to the President's private dining area—well away from the press and reporters—by John Ashley.

"I was told, quite directly, by the President to escort you here and then leave," Ashley said.

He knocked on the door. Both men heard, "Come in." With that, Ashley shook Hull's hand and told him, "Good luck. Stay safe," which Hull found strange.

Hull had almost forgotten what dress clothes felt like. After his customary hot and cold shower, he looked into the locker where his new clothes had been placed. Reviewing his options, he selected a pair of dark tan slacks with a light blue dress shirt, unbuttoned at the throat.

Slowly, he extracted the box he had mailed to Chasey before departing for Tibet. Fortunately, Chasey had the foresight to bring it with him when summoned to bring Hull home. Hull looked at his wallet, gazing fondly at a picture of his wife, Tamara, before placing it in his left rear pocket. The special SEAL watch he once shared with his friend, who had been executed in Oklahoma, slipped easily over his wrist. Lastly, he carefully removed his special sword, guarded in a silk sheath woven many years ago. Placing it between his shoulder blades left no identifiable bulge under his shirt.

Laughing to himself, he noticed the slacks were at least one size too large—thanks to the spartan diet offered by the monks. The remaining clothes included a full-dress United States Marine Corps officer's uniform, a Marine Corps field fatigue uniform, and a pair of blue denim jeans with matching boots. Hull's only complaint: normal dress shoes were extremely painful to wear at the moment. He was immediately put at ease when he noticed the President was wearing a tailored sweat suit and running shoes.

"Well, if I do say so, you look and smell one hell of a lot better than this morning," the President said as he rose to shake Hull's hand. "Be seated, relax. I ordered my special meal—one my doctor and wife detest the few times I'm able to have it. I took the liberty of ordering the same for you. That way, if I'm questioned, I can say you made a special request and I was just being polite. Gives me 'plausible deniability,'" Beatherd chuckled.

"Listen, I had six days to become familiar with your personality, achievements, military and non-military exploits—and some details from your father. Your favorite libation: Stoli, neat."

At the mention of the drink, a waiter in formal attire entered, presenting the President with his favorite Blanton's Single Barrel bourbon. The same waiter then served Hull a tumbler of clear liquid—Stolichnaya, as requested.

The alcohol caused Hull to catch his breath.

"I've only had tea to drink these past months," Hull confessed. "This drink brings back favorite memories—my father and I on our hunting expeditions, and later during my military service. Thank you for allowing me to use your personal workout facilities. Your valet assured me the mud and other residue found on my body would be washed down the drain with no resulting odor or sight." Hull smiled. "Would you mind if we discussed why you selected me to be your guest today while we eat? I can't understand why."

"Sure, no problem," Beatherd replied. "Other than the fact that I had no idea who you were until seven days ago, our country—and the entire world—might be in extreme danger of extinction from a threat unknown to any of our resources or even the best intelligence agencies in Russia and China. Both countries have suffered the same horrendous deaths as ours. The leaders of the special forces in both nations agreed you would be the perfect leader of a team to combat the unknown threat."

"Still unclear in my mind why I'm here," Hull said, still puzzled by the circumstances of his rapid departure from the monastery and sudden appearance, in rags, before the President.

"Ashley told me I have to keep you out of sight for national security reasons. I'll explain more later. For now, let's eat—I can hardly wait to share my favorite meal with you." Beatherd pressed a small button under his chair to alert the staff that it was time for the meal to be served.

Hull watched as the same server returned, this time carrying a large serving dish with the Presidential Seal etched on the cover. The server placed it in front of the President, then returned to the kitchen and soon came back with an identical dish, placing it before Hull.

"Permit me to do the honors," the President said while removing the cover. "And remember: 'plausible deniability,'" Beatherd laughed.

Hull surveyed the entrée before throwing his head back in loud, raucous laughter.

"Excuse me, Mr. President," he said, "I've never seen a hamburger this large—layered with Swiss cheese and smothered in French fries. Is that a chocolate shake?"

He now understood why Beatherd's wife and doctor would frown on his meal choices.

"Forgive my laughter. My lips are sealed," Hull said, following the President's lead in placing a few fries into his mouth without a fork.

Pausing between bites of fries, sips of shake, and bites of burger, Beatherd began, "What I'm about to tell you is *Top Secret*. China, Russia, and our country have all experienced deaths that cannot be identified—no one knows what killed them, who killed them, or worst of all, how they were killed."

Beatherd's expression turned grim as he drained the remains of his large shake.

"As I mentioned, I knew nothing about you until the Chinese and Russian Special Forces leaders mentioned you by name. The Chinese leader referred to you as 'Ghost Killer,' and the Russian leader demanded a rematch in some kind of vodka-drinking contest."

Now Beatherd paused, exhaling deeply, as though releasing a long-held burden.

Hull grinned, lips half open and curling at the corners of his mouth.

"Sir, to rephrase what you've told me—people are dying from an unknown cause, by parties you cannot determine, and delivered through unknown agents. You must have access to thousands of top intelligence agents who could solve this better than me."

"Perhaps," Beatherd replied. "But I doubt it. Once the Russians and Chinese agreed you were the ideal leader for a team to solve our mutual problem, I called in some old friends—Kenneth James, former head of the CIA, and Don Mangrum, former head of FBI

Intelligence. I've had previous discussions with them, and I wanted to use their knowledge and experience to identify someone capable of dealing with so many unknown variables. Without mentioning your name, they both told me individually that only *Roy Hull* stood any chance of dealing with the crisis confronting our nation."

12

History of Poison Gas

Bahia Blanca

Ernest Laboratory Meeting room

March 10

Hans Ernst reviewed the notes left by his grandfather and father detailing their efforts in converting a lethal gas—Zyklon B, used in concentration camps—into a liquid form. A liquid form was critical for delivering a lethal dosage to a known location without it evaporating.

His head pounded painfully from the long hours he was forced to work under the new Chancellor. The hours, days, weeks, and even months were rigidly enforced by the Chancellor's security force, headed by Kim Hickler, granddaughter of the infamous Richard Hickler.

Only last week, he recalled, one of his assistants told her the process could not be sped up to meet the increased demand. Without warning, she pulled her revolver and shot the assistant in the leg. Hans had wondered, how would shooting make the process go faster? He now understood why most people in the complex regarded Kim Hickler as a deranged but highly skilled assassin.

Hans examined his own notes while working to locate a new chemical agent capable of converting gaseous substances into liquid form. It had taken almost three years of experimentation to successfully combine two agents into a stable, demonstrable compound. The number of deaths resulting from testing—both human and animal—was a closely guarded secret within the complex.

Leafing through the notes, he had highlighted key dates:

- **15 August 1951** – His grandfather Ernst discovered the proper compound mixture to increase the gas's death potential.

- **1 October 2001** – A passage written by his father, Marcus, detailed the addition of a newly discovered protein. Using a highly specific distillation process, the gas was transformed into a plasma state, making it suitable for transportation.

He smiled to himself. The next date in the sequence was one he had written.

After years of research under immense pressure from the Chancellor's office, Hans had perfected a highly efficient delivery system with help from his friend— the grandson of the man who developed the V1 and V2 rocket systems during the war. The rocket expert, August Braun, had explained the use of GPS (Global

Positioning System) to target any location on Earth. Unknown to Hans, August had also been experimenting with drone technology. His prototype drones were remotely operated and designed with carbon fiber, rendering them invisible to radar—strong, stealthy, and costly.

Hans reread his notes about the delivery system for his lethal compound. He had tested several methods for transporting the weapon without losing effectiveness.

One of his favorite pastimes was competitive sports shooting. He often won against his friends, convinced that hand-loading his own ammunition gave him a significant edge. One evening, while preparing rounds for the next day's match, Hans had an idea: *Why couldn't a cartridge be made of plastic, filled with liquid, and used as a localized delivery system for death in open spaces?* The primer would ignite the liquid, triggering the deadly release.

The Chancellor had shared information about the weapon with only three of his closest allies—each head of a major defense-related enterprise. When Hans presented the invention to businessmen from Russia, China, and the United States, all three were skeptical. The Chinese delegate openly mocked the weapon in front of the others. However, the American and Russian representatives were intrigued enough to pay the Chancellor for a private, controlled demonstration.

13

Hull Gives Names to President

White House

Presidential Dining Area

2100 Hours

Hull noticed the President had finished all his fries and most of his burger, while he had left most of both uneaten.

"Your dinner menu is excellent, Mr. President, but after eating 'greens and grains' for the past few months, I'm taking it slow tonight," Hull said, hoping that was a good enough explanation for the President.

"Take your time. I have plenty to discuss with you while you finish your meal," Beatherd said, retrieving a file folder with "HULL" scrawled across the front. Opening the folder, the President selected a document with a red seal attached. He previewed the document before looking directly at Hull.

"This is a top-secret psyops file. Somehow, your father managed to obtain it. I didn't ask him how when I called him last week, and he didn't volunteer the information. I read both psychological profiles—one from when you entered the Naval Academy at age seventeen, and the other from when your father picked you up from that Buddhist monastery twenty-five years later. I read and reread both profiles, which are filled with notes on neural networks and synapses.

"I called in leading brain specialists and psychology experts. Their explanation left me even more perplexed. I also noticed your physical charts specified that you were only to be treated by Doctor Donna Running Deer. Your father confirmed she was—and still is—the only physician allowed to treat you for anything beyond a sprained ankle. John found she's currently the head of Johns Hopkins Hospital in Baltimore. She's a rear admiral and recently lost her husband in an accident in Oklahoma last year.

"She paid me a visit at my home last week, and I asked her what the two profiles indicated to her about you—and your fitness to lead this extremely sensitive covert operation."

Beatherd stopped and extracted a single sheet of plain paper, grinning as he handed it to Hull. "You can read what she wrote and told me."

Hull read Dr. Deer's cryptic comment to the President:

"HULL IS NOT WIRED LIKE ANY OTHER MORTAL. RECOVERING FROM A BITE BY A HIGHLY VENOMOUS SNAKE IN EARLY CHILDHOOD ENABLED HULL TO DO MENTAL AND PHYSICAL FEATS UNLIKE ANY OTHER

HUMAN BEING. HULL CANNOT USE NORMAL BLOOD TRANSFUSIONS AS THEY WOULD CAUSE HIM TO DIE WITHIN MINUTES."

He handed the folder back to the President, laughing. "A woman of few words—and my closest friend. I knew her late husband. I did my best in Oklahoma to make his death have a meaning."

"After discussing with Doctor Deer and reading her comment, John compiled a chronological index of your fitness reports while in the service. Now, personally, I never thought those reports were worth the paper they're written on. I changed my mind when I read yours.

'Exceptional' was the term used in every report—except one, which stated you should be immediately given a bad conduct discharge." Beatherd's face turned grim. "I asked John to look into that vast discrepancy. I also called my new friend—your father— and asked him why that one particular officer gave you such a poor report."

Beatherd's face convulsed with laughter. "Your father strung together so many four-letter words that my phone overheated and my ears rang. To summarize, he told me that the son of a bitch had your wife and infant daughter hacked to death in Iraq.

"Their deaths caused you to resign your commission, disappear into anonymity, and perform 'black ops' when directed by the President." Beatherd turned to Hull with a slight grin.

"My father's comments are painfully accurate," Hull replied. "All of my prior value systems vanished completely when I buried my wife and daughter. I went into darkness and became, as my Russian friend called me, 'the crazed one, a man without a soul.'

"I committed atrocities too numerous to mention, always feeling I was in the right. One morning, I woke up with blood covering my body, not knowing how it got there. The woman I was staying with started crying and told me I needed help. She drove me to the airport when I told her I needed to travel to a Buddhist monastery in Tibet—the one recommended to me many years ago by my friend, Donna Running Deer, at the funeral of my wife and daughter."

"That explains the long void in your service record," Beatherd said. "When your father found you and brought you to the VA for psychological therapy, they diagnosed you as completely normal. Your technical brilliance in liquid distribution systems led to your position as head of that new technology at the University of North Florida.

"During that time, you found your second wife—a most charming and gifted woman—Tamara. When I informed her we were meeting today, and that I would be putting you on a plane with armed guards, she flat-out warned me not to tell any of your friends or family until Saturday.

"Or," he added, laughing, "I think she was kidding—she said I wouldn't be alive to run for a second term. According to her, the two of you have a great deal of catching up to do."

"Mr. President, Tamara never jokes," Hull said. "Can you order up some extra-strong coffee? We have a great deal to discuss in a very short time. And thank you for the transportation offer, but I've made arrangements to fly back in my corporate jet."

Beatherd replied with a smile. "Well, yes I can, but my chef is mad at you. The coffee he gave you this morning was sent back for being too weak. He told me personally he dumped the entire bag into the next cup, which you deemed still weak—but acceptable. I'm not sure we have cups strong enough to hold what he'll brew tonight."

"Sir, after hearing what the nation—and perhaps the world—is facing, may I give you a list of people I require to have any chance of solving what is happening? I'll contact these individuals personally. Some work for the government, like Doctor Deer. Others work in foreign countries. Long and short, I trust them. I'll need funding and your approval to use some people who may not be seen as law-abiding citizens—here or in their own country."

Hull handed his list to the President.

"In addition, I need Ashley to schedule a meeting for late next week with Red Cell. He can tell them the meeting can be in California or here. They may be the only organization with the unique abilities to help me quantify the unknown number of variables we're facing."

"Your list will only be given to Ashley later tonight," Beatherd said. "He'll arrange funding using our Black Ops budget, used only by the military. If you need people on this list, go get them. Use my name if you run into trouble with government officials.

"Saving our country is more important than a second term. One more thing I didn't mention earlier—Russia and China trust you, but not me. They insisted that one member from their special forces be part of your team." Beatherd took a small breath, waiting for Hull's reply.

He didn't have to wait long. Taking back the paper with the names he had previously given the President, Hull added two names to the list.

"Tell Ashley I want the people I need standing with me in front of the White House at 1300 hours Monday." He handed the paper back to Beatherd. "I'm ready for that special coffee now, Mr. President. Something tells me I'd better bring my 'A' game when I see Tamara."

"Hull, before you leave—what in the hell is Red Cell, and what makes it such a unique organization?" The President looked genuinely puzzled.

"Plausible deniability," Hull replied with a large smile on his face.

14

Bahia Blanca Drones and Poison

Bahia Blanca Argentina

Ernst Laboratory

March 11

August, the new delivery date for the next test is impossible to meet. I may draw the ire of Hickler. She will shoot me to show my staff that no excuse will be tolerated, Hans Ernst said with morbid humor.

August searched through his notes. "I've been toying with some changes to our basic delivery system. Your design of a thin plastic cartridge, with liquid gas ready to be released upon impact with a hard surface, was brilliant. Coupled with the GPS installed in each drone, it enables unprecedented control of a small delivery system. The combination has served us well in previous tests. The gas is potent enough to last ten minutes in outdoor conditions.

"For a test on a much larger scale than what we've handled before, I've made changes to both the size of the drone and the poison gas cartridge. Working with my staff, we've designed and built a fleet of much larger stealth drones. Using your basic concept, I replicated a shotgun shell which allows for a significantly larger payload. By adding a primer and sufficient powder to propel the projectile, I increased the payload by a factor of four.

"The powder is of my own design. When fired, the same blue bolt as before trails the cartridge. But I've saved the best for last, Hans. Each drone can now carry eight of the new, heavier cartridges. I've also installed a small telescope and camera on each unit. You now have the power to eliminate hundreds—maybe thousands— with a single drone.

"A larger fleet equipped with this deadly package will ensure that the next test frightens nations into procuring very expensive defensive systems from your associates. I'll have them ready for Hickler in seven days. She can ship them to her contacts for deployment. It will be her decision when to activate."

"August, that is outstanding—designing a larger drone to carry eight of the large cartridges, each under the control of a drone operator. Using the telescope and camera, the operator can position the drone over the largest group of people on the ground. Those capabilities will give them a most painful death."

Hans couldn't contain his emotions and danced around the laboratory.

15

Arrival of Jaz

Front Steps White House

March 20

1250 Hours

adMan, I am freezing, Chasey whispered to Colonel Michael Diana. Scanning the faces of the other Hull recruits, he concluded his discomfort was shared by the entire group. "When I picked up our Chinese partner last night, he had volunteered for this mission. The only information given to him was to report to a man named Hull in Washington, D.C. His name is John Tsia—he's not much for conversation. Now he's freezing with the rest of us, unlike Hull, who's wearing a short-sleeved blue T-shirt. Is it just my imagination, or does Hull look tired to you?"

Diana muffled a laugh. "Hull is waiting for the last volunteer from Russia. His instructions, I understand, stated quite specifically that the agent be here no later than 1300 hours. By my watch, that gives the Russian less than ten minutes to be standing in front of Hull."

Diana, Chasey, and the other members of Hull's select group all turned their heads down Pennsylvania Avenue, unsure of what was creating the loud, overpowering noise vibrating in their ears. Speeding toward the White House, a large number of enormous motorcycles rapidly approached Hull and the others.

The two lead bikers braked just feet from where Hull stood in front of his team. The biker closest to Hull removed their helmet, revealing a flowing mane of long, jet-black hair. She shook her hair loose, then walked slowly over to her companion, whose helmet identified him as *Terrible Tom*. She leaned in and kissed him several times.

"Thank you for escorting me to Washington. I look forward to seeing you after my assignment here is completed."

With that, Terrible Tom started his motorcycle and signaled the others to follow.

The female biker, dressed entirely in black leather, scanned the assembled men and women and walked directly toward Hull.

"Senior Spetsnaz Captain Jasymne Paristovk, reporting for duty. I take it you are Roy Hull, as everyone else is sensibly clothed—except you. My friends call me 'Jaz.' Other than that you can consume vast quantities of vodka, I know nothing about you or why I'm here."

Hull shook her hand. "Yes, I am Hull. I asked for you by name after discussing the qualities and abilities required for this mission.

Follow me to our temporary meeting room. You and the other members of this unique task force will be briefed on what we know to date and why you are here."

Hull turned to Ashley for directions.

"Stop," Jaz commanded, locking eyes with Hull. "I need shelter for my ride. I was ordered to meet you while enjoying a short holiday with Tom and my friends. The only clean clothes I have are bundled on my bike. You'll have to buy me new clothes, or the rest of you will not desire to be in the same room with me."

Chasey and Diana looked at each other in amusement. No one, other than his wife Tamara, had ever spoken to Hull in that tone.

Hull, never at a loss for words, replied, "Give me your keys. I'll ride it back to the parking area reserved for the Capitol Police Force. Your lack of clothes can wait until I meet with all of you. If you'd feel better, I can place you downwind of the others."

Jaz laughed while handing Hull her keys.

Ashley led the team across the White House grounds, all eyes glued to Hull, gliding effortlessly toward the parking garage in his short-sleeved T-shirt despite the freezing temperatures.

"As I told the President, Hull is not wired like other mortals," Ashley said quietly to MadMan. "It may be the snake blood coursing through his veins. After all these years of knowing him, I've never completely understood him." He shook his head in comic agreement.

Ashley opened the door to a windowless room. Only MadMan recognized it as a SCIF—Sensitive Compartmented Information Facility—designed to maintain complete secrecy in speech and electronics.

Hull entered and spoke in his patented, deep-based military voice. "Everybody get comfortable; I have to explain the unexplainable to you. Not everyone here knows each other."

He began the introductions.

"My name is Roy G. Hull. From my left to right: Morgan McGrath, Deputy Assistant in the CIA; Barbara Bonnie Peters, Senior FBI Agent; Harrison Blake, Senior FBI Agent; Colonel Michael Diana—answers to 'MadMan'; Dan Chasey, my companion on too many dangerous missions to count; John Tsia, Chinese PLA Special Operations; and last, but certainly not least, Jaz—" he paused, handing her keys back, "—on loan from the Russian Spetsnaz Special Forces. I am attempting to add my very good friend and computer specialist, Willi Peptovitch, as my current adviser is presently imprisoned in one of Russia's worst penal institutions."

"Hull, we've all been in deadly situations. What's so different about this one?" Jaz asked, her silky-smooth soprano calm but probing.

"I have to explain what I know—which is very little." Hull took a deep breath, organizing thoughts he'd reviewed countless times.

Stepping to the whiteboard at the front of the room, he wrote:

Multiple horrific deaths in each of our countries.

Cause of deaths medically impossible.

No detectable delivery system.

"All I can share with you is written on the board. At this time, we have no idea which unknown country or countries stand to benefit. The best I can tell you is we are going to battle a faceless, deadly enemy."

Hull rubbed his eyes, clearly perplexed by the gravity of the situation.

Ashley stood. "Most of you are likely exhausted from your long journeys here. I've arranged a series of rooms close to the CIA. You're scheduled to meet me tomorrow in one of their special training rooms. Jaz, if you'll follow me, I'll lead you to the hotel. Everyone else, a bus is waiting for you. All your expenses are covered. Looks like we all need a good night's sleep."

16

Parris Alpha Takes Action

Alpha Dynamics

Allen Parris, CEO Office

March 22, 0500 Hours

Parris seldom celebrated his victories with anything more than a slight grin and perhaps a second cup of ginseng tea imported directly from Sri Lanka, formerly known as Ceylon. He massaged the list of names associated with the pictures taken by one of his newly placed spies in the White House. Names were easy to find once Parris used his vast computer skills—both legal and illegal—not only to learn their identities but also to obtain technical, family, and financial information, all of which could prove helpful in the future.

The photos contained two individuals he could not identify, and a third image showed a man in a T-shirt riding a motorcycle, his back to the camera. He would use "Genius" to transmit the names and pictures after he had time to think about his next move.

Ashley was obviously the team leader. Parris realized Ashley had to be dealt with soon. Ashley was dictating a much more conservative and slower approach to funding in response to the newly emerging deadly threat facing the country. His informant mentioned a possible bidders' conference open to all high-tech companies. Perhaps, Parris smiled to himself, the next round of deaths would force them to act more rapidly.

Holding "Genius," Parris captured the photographs and the list of names. He hit the transmit key, sending the information to his fellow conspirators. The identities of the two unknown individuals might possibly be uncovered by his friends. The limited information relayed to Parris indicated this was a special team formed by the President. Only the President and Ashley knew its true function.

Parris's first thought was to contact Hickler and have her military team deal with the problem. He stopped short of calling her. He knew from experience about her exorbitant charges, and the fact that he had previously used a local organized criminal syndicate to remove competition. Parris knew he could not afford delays that would slow his funding. His instructions to the syndicate included names, pictures, and the promise of a bonus if all the individuals—especially Ashley—met a violent death.

His "Genius" device alerted him to an incoming message from his Russian friend, Victor Novak. A name was followed by a picture. The notes included a plea from Novak for Parris to contact Hickler and arrange for the timely death of the individual shown in the photo. Further explanation detailed how the man was delaying several billions of rubles from being authorized to Novak's organization. The message also listed the number of security guards protecting the target. It would require an assassin of extraordinary skill to eliminate this obstacle. The price upon completion: two million euros.

Parris picked up his phone, dialing a number used only for occasions requiring the highest level of security.

"I want to order today's special and have it delivered, please. Payment authorization is upon delivery."

Parris opened his laptop, using the retina scan to access the encrypted message section. Using predetermined protocols, he entered the details provided by Novak and addressed them to Kim Hickler. He hit send, knowing the network protocols he had developed would transmit the message through multiple international relays before reaching its final destination: a remote town in Argentina, Fuerth.

17

Secret Weapons Delivered

CIA Building

Special Operations SCIF room

March 27

Hull had Chasey place the newly purchased revolvers in front of each team member.

"Before you is the latest and most deadly sidearm available to any nation, country, or individual. Known as the *Pit Viper,* it requires weight balancing to best fit your height and weight. As comfortable as I am with weapons of all types, I realized the power and accuracy of this weapon when practicing last night."

Hull picked up his weapon while speaking to his team.

"I chose it as our weapon of choice to meet any unknown situations we may encounter. With a common weapon, our maintenance and ammunition problems will be reduced to a minimum. Your personal sidearms can remain as part of your protection, but they must be carried in a manner that does not hinder your movement with the *Pit Viper.*

"Our longer-range weapons are currently being tested. Again, not fully understanding the threat we face, there may be different weapons—all with the same caliber for uniformity.

"The shocking news is that only three of our team can train on the new revolver today due to lack of space and instructors. Chasey, Peters, and Blake have the morning shift. MadMan, Tsia, and I will take the afternoon session. Jaz, you and Running Deer have the evening session. When you're not training, I want all of you to continue your regular training regime. Set your watches. Training starts at 0830."

Jaz turned to Donna and said, "We can do the shopping we talked about and then have lunch today. I need clothes for every occasion. What better way than to have your government pay for them?" She laughed so hard at the thought, tears welled in her eyes.

Hull could see and hear Jaz laughing.

"What is so hilarious?" he asked, perturbed at the idea of anyone joking with so many unknown dangers ahead. He snapped, "What's so damn funny when people are dying?"

Donna was quick to defend Jaz.

"Both of us were rushed from our normal lives with no chance to pack any decent clothes. Jaz was just delighted she could select some clothing of various types and have Ashley pay for it. I feel the same way. I came here based on a phone call saying you needed my assistance immediately. I can tell you—I need some new clothes.

We don't know how long it will take to find a solution. You can't expect us to be wearing winter clothing in the summer, can you?"

Laughing uncharacteristically, Hull replied, "I have just the partner for your shopping expedition. My wife vowed I would be a single man if I left her for any extended time. She mentioned something about shopping, since we—or rather, she—live primarily in Florida. Donna, you know Tamara. Take her cell number and call her. She'll be delighted to have you two as shopping companions."

"I'll call Tam and invite her to go shopping with us. We learned there's a large shopping mall within walking distance. If time allows, we'll stop and have lunch—and charge it to Ashley's account."

Donna and Jaz couldn't leave the room fast enough, laughing as they opened and closed the door.

MadMan and Chasey remained seated. The others had departed.

"Roy, have a seat," Chasey said. "MadMan and I have questions about one of your team. If our backs aren't covered, we could all end up dead—or worse. The FBI folks are trained and resourceful. We've observed John's training routine. He has command of several weapons and can fight hand-to-hand. He's a good guy to have on our side.

"You grew up with Donna. You're confident that, with training, she can provide adequate backup, or she wouldn't be on our team.

But Jaz poses a problem for us. We never see her train—either in our facilities or outdoors. She may be a weak link in our armor."

Chasey had been friends with Hull for too many years not to ask the tough questions.

Hull took a sip from his ever-present coffee mug.

"I understand what you're saying. My attention has been mostly devoted to Ashley and my wife since we got here. Since I can confide in you both, let me explain: my demands for agents from other countries were extremely detailed when it came to their capabilities and training.

"From my Chinese contact, I required someone with deep diving capabilities—since I may need a partner if our threat comes from the sea or any large body of water. From the Russians, I wanted someone capable of working alone in high-stress situations with one important specialty: killing.

"If we find out what's causing the problems, I don't want to leave it operational.

"Dan, don't be late for your training session. Like all of us, you need to learn how to use all the options available to us.

"MadMan, reach out to Tsia and ask if anything strange has occurred in his country. I have a meeting with Ashley to arrange a briefing with the Red Cell members."

18

Ashley and Hull

CIA Building

John Ashley's conference room

March 27, 1030 Hours

The CIA building reminded Hull of President Truman's insistence on renaming the World War II intelligence service from the OSS to the CIA—mainly due to the OSS sounding too similar to the Nazi SS. Ashley had told him this was the room where the President received most of his top-secret briefings. The building and room allowed for greater security and limited access.

The room was furnished with a floor-to-ceiling television screen, several smaller televisions, a landline phone, and outlets for laptop computers. Hull was studying the instructions given to him when Ashley came into view.

"Nobody ever finds their destination in this place the first time," Ashley said. "My secretary informed me you'd left the training room, which meant you could be wandering around for hours—or I could track you down and make your passage easier. Follow me. We're close, but my meeting room is tucked into a corner."

Ashley grinned at Hull while stepping briskly into his somewhat hidden meeting room.

"Forgive me," Ashley said, taking out his government-issued cell phone. "Fred, forgive me. I had to take my wife's car in for service today without notifying you. Can you please pick up my attaché case from my wife? I just had a lapse of memory and forgot to take it with me. When you arrive, bring it to my private meeting room at the CIA.

"Between you and me, I think the Commanders will draft a cornerback in the upcoming draft. I know you believe it'll be a wide receiver. Our normal lunch bet—who pays, to the winner."

Ashley slid the phone into his coat pocket while speaking to Hull.

"Fred has been my driver and good friend since the first day he picked me up from my home. We're both avid pro football fans and discuss—sometimes argue—the best options for our home team.

"After perusing your history for the President, I was astounded that you were twice named an All-American defensive back while at the Naval Academy. You carried a very odd nickname, Roy— 'The Ninja Hull.'

"As many of your teammates are still on active duty, I took the liberty of calling one or two. I had to hold back a laugh when Fred

Reynold, who played wide receiver, enlightened me. He said it was your head coach who tagged you 'The Ninja,' explaining that he told the offensive players: *Hull comes from nowhere, makes a vicious hit, and escapes to do it again.*"

"Fred also told me the same coach wouldn't allow you to participate in live scrimmages anymore because you were literally injuring your own teammates. Being unable to play in future games didn't endear you to the coaches—or your teammates. Knowing that helps me better understand your actions. Top speed, all-out, all the time seems to be your trademark, echoed by the teammates I contacted."

Ashley couldn't hide a grin as he spoke.

"Some of my most memorable days," Hull smiled.

"I called my contacts at Red Cell. They've arranged for team members to meet at one of the executive screening rooms in forty-eight hours. They're always up for the challenge of creating new ways to simulate deadly actions.

"The first time I met with them, they explained how the group was formed. Apparently, neither the CIA, NSA, nor FBI had ever contemplated terrorists crashing jetliners into office buildings—like what happened on 9/11.

"Government agencies have a hard time thinking outside the box, but people who make their living imagining new and unique scenarios of danger and death don't suffer from those mental restrictions. Producers, directors, screenwriters, stunt men and women, and even some actors and actresses participate in these highly classified intelligence sessions."

"The President agrees with our strategy of not allocating any special funding for the current problem until the DOD can draw up a list of requirements to present at a bidders' conference in the coming weeks," Ashley said as he scanned his notes.

"Your friend in the Russian jail, Willi Pepovitch, presented me with a bigger problem. The President choked on his coffee when I mentioned you needed him. When I told him Willi was in a Russian prison and that I needed two million dollars to bail him out, Betherd looked at me like I'd lost all mental faculties.

"He finally agreed when I explained that you believe Willi could be instrumental in finding the source of the threat. I called your contact Boris three times to bribe him for Willi's release. He laughed at me."

Ashley looked and sounded frustrated by his lack of success.

"Yes, I need him to deal with the data techniques and equipment we believe are part of the unknown operation," Hull replied. He reached for the desk phone with a speaker and began dialing.

Speaking in Russian, Hull's conversation was unintelligible to Ashley until Hull told the other party they must continue in English for Ashley's benefit.

"Boris, my good friend," Hull said. "Ashley tells me you refused two million American dollars to free Willi."

Hull listened intently as Boris explained the many problems he faced as prison director in releasing Willi. Hull's eyes narrowed, and his face tightened.

"Boris, you know better than most how upset I become when a good friend refuses a bribe. Let me put it to you another way: either take the money and arrange for Willi to be freed—or in forty-eight hours, I will have my sword at your neck."

Ashley heard Boris reply: "That would be an idle threat from anyone but you. I know your talent with the blade. Place your comrade on the phone so I can give him detailed instructions on the transfer of my money."

Alpha Dynamics

Office of Max Parris

1100 Hours

Max Parris closed his office door. He wanted no interference while speaking to the criminals he had hired.

"Between eleven and one is an excellent window. Eliminating all outside personnel brought in to interfere with the plan is a business necessity. If you can, leave a bloody warning—a bonus goes to each one who draws blood."

Parris placed the phone back on the receiver, congratulating himself on a plan well organized and under budget.

19

Jaz in Action

Angelo's Italian Restaurant

Prestige Mall

Langley Va

1230 Hours

If I had one more bite of a cannoli, I wouldn't fit into the new slacks I just purchased, Tamara Hull laughed as they left the restaurant with her two new friends. "Roy being absent for eight months was difficult—both mentally and physically. I worried constantly. His mother and father consoled me, reminding me he had been absent for over fifteen years after the death of his first wife. Donna's frequent calls kept my spirits up. She insisted Roy was in great shape when the two of them met in Oklahoma, during that vain attempt to save Donna's husband.

"The best and worst part of my husband is his unique moral and mental code. He sees no gray—just black and white. It was a pleasure to have him return, aside from his dining habits. One meal a day and plenty of coffee was more than enough for me to perform my CEO duties at the hedge fund I manage with Roy's mother. But Roy insisted we have three meals a day. He requires protein and calories to replenish the energy used in his three hours a day of martial arts training. We had to renovate our condo to include all the training equipment he uses."

"I'm having difficulty moving," Donna Running Deer groaned. "What a spectacular lunch to top off a great time shopping." Donna had been reclusive since the recent death of her husband. Her only comfort came in knowing her childhood friend, Roy Hull, had avenged his death. "Tamara, if it's any consolation, Roy has always had that little-sleep, high-activity lifestyle he exhibits today. I did many studies and always reached the same conclusion. The snakebite he suffered when he was very young gave him extraordinary physical and mental capabilities—unlike any other human. His concept of right and wrong is definitely unique."

Jaz was unexpectedly talkative, which went against her training.

"What a pleasure to have our clothes and other items delivered to our hotel. We must all thank Ashley for letting us charge everything to his White House account. Once we flashed that White House credit card, the stores couldn't do enough for us." Her laughter was infectious, and the other women laughed along with her.

"Did you actually dance with the Bolshoi Ballet, or were you just teasing Donna and me at lunch? Your slender body would certainly be suitable for ballet. But your current occupation—being part of one of the most feared special forces units in the world—makes that idea almost laughable," Tam said, looking directly at Jaz with a slightly amused expression.

"What if I told you I still dance with them when the need arises?" Jaz replied, smiling. "I was twelve and had been a student with the Bolshoi for two years when the Spetsnaz needed a different type of courier for delivering highly sensitive information. The type of data that, if discovered by a foreign law enforcement agency, would mean instant death—no questions asked.

"But no law enforcement agency ever suspects members of the ballet to be anything but artists. Due to my father's military background, they had me perform a series of physical tests. To my surprise, I was selected over a number of women dancers and athletes. Bolshoi administrators were informed I would be training with the Spetsnaz. If my dancing skills were needed, I could return and train with them. The military experience has created a dual nature in me. I can be sweet and sour within seconds."

"That would describe Roy Hull," Donna Running Deer said, smiling at the memory. "I grew up with him. Being from a Native American family, I was constantly harassed and bullied by the white logging kids. More than once, Roy stepped in to defend me. His martial arts training from the age of three came in useful. After a few bloody noses and broken arms, the logging kids kept a safe distance from me, knowing I had a small enforcer as my defender.

"His father was just as protective. Prejudiced adults would taunt and laugh at the Native Americans in town. Roy's grandmother—his mother's mother—was a Native American and the principal of our school. Roy and his father were instrumental in helping me become a doctor.

"And Roy—never to be mentioned—is a world-renowned concert pianist who performs under an alias. In fact, when he was at the Academy, he had special permission to leave for weekend concerts. His concert earnings paid for the expenses my scholarship didn't cover.

"In my last year, my advisor wouldn't advance me to the cardiology specialty because I refused to sleep with him. I called Roy and cried on the phone about what was happening. A few days later, Roy's father showed up on campus. I had no idea he was coming. That night at dinner, he told me my advisor had changed his decision, and I would be studying cardiology. It wasn't until the next summer, when I returned home and spoke with Roy, that I learned his father had a one-on-one discussion with my advisor—more or less telling him that if he didn't change my specialty, it might be his last day on earth." Donna always enjoyed recalling that story.

"It's only twelve fifteen. We can take a more leisurely pace back to the CIA classroom. I enjoy the sun after all these gloomy days," Tamara said, a true Florida woman. Jaz and Donna agreed, until Jaz noticed something out of the corner of her left eye—something her Spetsnaz training had imprinted into her subconscious.

"Tam and Donna, walk a little faster. When we arrive at the street corner, take a hard right and keep walking. It may be nothing, but two men were gazing intently at us in the restaurant. Now they're walking directly behind us, closing the distance. Until I'm satisfied, stay behind me. Turn now and keep walking," Jaz commanded, her tone alarming Donna and Tamara.

Jaz stayed hidden by the building, waiting for the two men to pass. A few seconds later, both men turned the corner, following the three women. It wasn't until each reached for a large knife that Jaz sprang into action.

Confronting the man closest to her, she executed a leaping kick into his groin. He collapsed at her feet, moaning and cursing. The second man, seeing what had happened to his partner, savagely attacked Jaz with his knife—only to realize that she had pivoted and was now holding a Spetsnaz-issued close-combat dagger in her hand. He barely saw it before she plunged it into his chest, muffling his screams with her other hand.

The first man, curled into a fetal position, never felt Jaz's blade slit his windpipe.

"Ladies, I feel it's best we hurry along to our CIA classroom," Jaz said softly.

Both Donna and Tamara stood wide-eyed in astonishment at Jaz as they quickly moved to obey.

20

Attacked

White House

John Ashley conference room

1240 Hours

I will free your Russian hacker from his prison. What I will tell the President is partly your message and partly fiction. How about grabbing some lunch? I'm starved, Ashley said, asking Hull more out of politeness than necessity—he was going to eat regardless of Hull's answer.

Hull nodded in agreement, and both men headed for the door. Before they could leave, the door burst open and one of Ashley's assistants rushed in, screaming, "Turn on the TV, sir! You have to see this!"

He turned on the television, which was set to a local station by default. Before their eyes, a cloud of smoke and fire erupted on the screen, shooting fifty feet or more into the air.

"That must have been some accident," Ashley commented. "Why did you think it was important for us to see?"

"Sir, that was your limo that exploded. According to the commentary, there were no survivors."

Ashley quickly dialed Fred's personal number. He frowned. "It went straight to voicemail."

Only seconds passed before Hull's phone diverted his attention from the screen.

"Roy, this is Chasey. Something terrible has happened. Blake and Peters—they've been shot while running during our noon break. I was behind them. My new revolver needed some fine-tuning, so I left after them.

An ambulance is on-site. Peters's wound doesn't appear to be severe. Blake's injuries are much worse. For some unknown reason, after shooting him, they picked up his bloody body. The big guy kept hitting him. I fired a shot, which made the three men flee.

The driver said the best hospital for these kinds of wounds is Johns Hopkins, and it's only about forty minutes away. I'm riding in the ambulance with them. Blake needs the best doctors you can round up. I'll see you at the hospital."

Ashley noticed Hull's face turn stoic—no muscle movement, no expression.

"Apparently, our team has been compromised," Hull said. "Dan Chasey reported our two FBI agents were shot. It now appears you're on the same hit list as my team." He turned to face Ashley. "You'd better increase security for both yourself and the President.

I have to worry about my wife, my friend, and Jaz. They were out on a shopping trip this morning. Forgive me, but I have to go find them."

Hull didn't wait for Ashley's response. He ran through the open door.

CIA employees weren't used to seeing a large man weaving and dodging through the hallways like a linebacker. Once outside, Hull sprinted like he was about to score the winning touchdown.

He entered the vacant classroom, the memories of not being able to protect his first wife, Ashley, gnawing at him. Then he heard resounding laughter that made him pause.

Standing at the entrance were Jaz, Donna, MadMan, and his wife Tamara. It was Tamara's laughter that filled him with relief and gratitude.

Walking over to join them, he asked, "What's so funny?"

MadMan, grinning broadly, replied, "Two men tried to injure or kill these three ladies. Tamara said both are now dead thanks to Jaz. The reason we're laughing is because of Tamara's description—she said if one of them had survived, he'd be singing soprano for the rest of his life."

Even Hull couldn't help but laugh at his wife's vivid and humorous retelling.

"You were lucky," he said, turning serious. "Peters and Blake were ambushed while running. Chasey is with them on the way to Johns Hopkins.

MadMan, stay with Jaz and Tamara. Donna, from what Chasey told me, one or both are going to need your special skills."

21

Update

Johns Hopkins Hospital

Baltimore Maryland

1430 Hours

Roy, how did you manage to get a police escort to my hospital? We made record time. Flying through those red lights was something I've always wanted to do, Donna said, choking back a laugh. "Let me check on our patients and scrub up. The attending ER physician is a good friend of mine.

What I've learned so far is that Peters was lucky—bloody, but with only slight damage. Blake's gunshot wounds aren't fatal, but something is causing internal bleeding. The on-duty surgeon is in the middle of the operation now and will probe to figure out the source. Trust me, I'll be ready to take over if I feel it's necessary."

She turned away and gave Hull their customary childhood greeting: "He catches them, I skin them."

Hull smiled. "Friends in high places," he said, watching Donna run down the hall.

"This is just a scratch," FBI Agent Peters told Chasey, struggling to remove the restraints that were limiting her movement.

Chasey, known as Mr. Five-by-Five due to his broad, stocky build, didn't say anything to reassure her. "You lost a lot of blood. If I'd been five minutes later, both of you would've been nothing more than press clippings and statistics."

A loud knock on Peters's hospital door announced Hull's entry. "Peters, you look like a mummy with all those bandages wrapped around your head." Hull tried to inject a little humor into the situation, but he could tell immediately it only irritated her more.

"If it's not too painful, can you describe what happened?"

"She can't, but I can," Chasey interrupted. "The three of us agreed to go for a run after class. My Pit Viper needed some adjustment to fit my hands better, so Blake and Peters started out while I stayed behind. I told them I'd catch up. I don't know why they laughed, but I was gaining on them.

I was about ten minutes behind when three men jumped out of a moving car. They ran up behind Blake and Peters. One man shot Peters once. I saw the blood pouring from her head as she hit the ground. The other two shot Blake multiple times. He crumpled to the pavement—badly wounded or maybe dead, I couldn't tell.

Then the man who shot Peters started yelling something at the others. They picked Blake up and held him while the first man beat him several times. I drew my personal Glock and fired over their heads. There were civilians nearby, so I couldn't risk aiming at them directly—but it was enough to scare them off."

"Wait. I swear I heard those men say, 'These are the two FBI agents we need to finish,'" Peters interrupted. "Even while I was lying on the ground, I heard them call one of the men 'ape' and say something else that sounded like 'Fopuna,' aimed at the guy who was beating Blake.

Chasey showed up just in time, and the three of them disappeared. Hull, they knew who we were."

"Too much to be a coincidence," Hull said. "Just before I came here, Tamara, Donna, and Jaz were targeted in an attack by two men. Jaz neutralized them—no harm done. Then Ashley's government-assigned car was blown up, killing his driver. I was in his office when it happened. I told him to get home and protect his family.

Peters, you mentioned hearing a word like 'Fopuna.' Did it sound like a foreign word?"

Peters gave a tired laugh. "I was shot, bleeding, and lying on the ground—but yeah, your pronunciation was what I heard. My head is throbbing. Hand me that glass of water—and let me sleep."

Hull and Chasey stepped into the hallway.

"No need for instructions," Chasey said. "I won't leave her side until someone relieves me, Roy."

"We've been combat buddies for too long," Hull said with a laugh. "I wasn't going to ask you to stay with Peters. I knew you would, no matter what. I'm just waiting for Donna to finish the surgery. I'll text her to meet me in the cafeteria when she's done."

Hull shook Chasey's hand and headed down the hall toward the cafeteria.

22

Evil Located

Johns Hopkins Hospital

Cafeteria

1800 Hours

People milled about the cafeteria, their conversations muted, creating a kind of audio blanket. Food and drinks were essential before visiting friends receiving care. Hull found a vacant table in the back. Artificial lighting reflected off the back walls.

He was deep in thought, replaying the words Peters had heard. His background in multiple languages assured him that the word she heard—"ape"—was the Serbian word for it. The way it was shouted, full of adrenaline, revealed the attacker's nationality. Hull had no current intelligence on where Serbians lived, worked, or socialized in the area. Jaz, having lived in Eastern Europe, would likely have better information. He dialed her cell and left a detailed voicemail message.

Stirring his coffee, his mind began sorting and connecting the facts. Ashley's limo had been destroyed by a well-placed explosive.

Peters and Blake were shot at nearly the same time. And shortly after, Jaz had defended Donna and Tamara from an ambush. These incidents led Hull to two alarming conclusions.

First, their team had been identified by enemies who would stop at nothing to eliminate them. Second, it was now his responsibility to move them into a secure position. As he calculated his options, MadMan pulled up a chair beside him.

"I'm always glad to see you, but who's guarding Tam and Jaz?" Hull asked.

"Have no fear," MadMan replied with his usual laugh. "Tamara's in excellent hands. Donna was scheduled for 'Pit Viper' training this afternoon with Jaz, but I took your wife and Jaz to the training area reserved for our team. Tamara, filling in for Donna, was first up for training—even though she'll probably never carry the weapon.

She surprised me—not only did she know how to shoot, but she shot very well. She told me your daughter taught her how to handle a revolver. After seeing her marksmanship, I told the instructor to fit her with a Pit Viper, and that you'd handle the paperwork when you got back."

Now it was Hull's turn. "This isn't for public consumption, but my sweet wife has had to shoot—and kill—on at least three occasions to protect herself. Tish, my daughter, keeps reminding me

Tamara can handle herself. But knowing that doesn't make me worry any less."

"I'm saving the best part of the shooting session for last," MadMan said, unable to contain his laughter. "Jaz took her position facing the target while the instructor began explaining the new weapon. She took it, racked a round, told us to put on our ear protection, and then placed all ten rounds dead center. The instructor was stunned.

She took a second clip from him and did it again—ten more rounds in the black. You should've seen the look on his face. He took off his hearing protection, told her she didn't need any more training, and handed her the external hardware package. Jaz told him she'd fired the weapon in both training and combat.

Tamara and I agreed—those two can more than defend themselves. Makes me feel kind of expendable," he chuckled. "John Tsia and I wanted to see Peters and Blake. We borrowed a staff car using Ashley's name to get here. I left John with Chasey. Didn't want to disturb Peters's sleep."

"Let me bounce some thoughts off you," Hull said. "Our team may be at the beginning stage of a full-blown military-style operation. If I'm right, we're going to need advanced planning and logistical support. We have to accept that our team has been compromised. Only Tam and I may still be unknown to whoever is trying to kill us."

Hull finished, still uncertain whether he'd accounted for all the complex variables.

"Look what I found in the hallway," Dan Chasey announced as he entered with Doctor Running Deer, still in her surgical scrubs, her arm around his.

Hull noticed she looked drawn—but not tired.

"I wanted to give you my report on Blake before I head back to recovery," Donna said slowly. Her clothes had been changed, though there were still specks of blood on her forehead and in her hair.

"He'll need 24-hour monitoring for the foreseeable future. The gunshot wounds missed any vital organs. The real damage came from the beating. Multiple fractures—most notably to the skull—caused swelling of the brain. The next three to four days will be critical.

My staff moved a second bed into his room. I'll stay with him. If I need to step away, I'll make sure Blake has the best medical support available. When Chasey told me Blake had been shot and was bleeding—then picked up by two men so a third, more muscular man could beat him—I couldn't comprehend it. Honestly, I still can't."

She rose to leave, but not before meeting Hull's gaze.

Chasey, MadMan, and Donna all recognized the signs. Hull's eyes narrowed, his nostrils flared, and his breathing slowed. He was preparing for battle. Plain and simple.

Hull's phone rang. It was Jaz, responding to the message he'd left earlier. He repeated the name back to her to confirm he'd heard it correctly.

"Dan and MadMan, I need you to guard Blake's room until I can arrange replacements I trust," he instructed. "Donna can get you both comfortable chairs. Make yourselves visible to staff and any visitors."

"Does that mean you won't be here?" MadMan asked.

"Plausible deniability," Hull replied, standing and walking toward the exit. "Donna loaned me her new Jag. I've got unfinished business."

23

Belgrade Fortress

The Belgrade Fortress

Washington D.C.

2100 Hours

Jaz had informed Hull that "The Fort" had become a favorite gathering spot for young Serbian men and women. It featured a combination gym and bar in separate areas, connected by a door.

Spotting a parking space close to the front door, Hull parked Donna's prized possession—her new Jaguar F-Type R75—a safe distance from any other vehicles. Should the three men he was searching for not be in the gym or bar, he would be forced to continue his search another time.

Clear glass windows at the front of the gym gave passersby a shadowy view of men and women using the facilities. Pulling the wool cap over his head, Hull stopped in front of the gym, scanning for the likeness of the three men described by Chasey. He couldn't be certain, but three men using the bench press equipment matched the mental image Chasey had given. He opened the front door for a clearer, more focused appraisal.

The three men using the bench press were clearly in good spirits—laughing out loud, shouting curses, and congratulating themselves on a job well done. Hull began forming an action plan in the back of his mind.

The attendant behind the counter asked Hull if he wanted to work out this evening. He hadn't changed from his jeans and short-sleeved T-shirt worn at that morning's meeting.

"No," Hull said, peeling off a hundred-dollar bill. "This is yours if you'll turn off your security cameras for fifteen minutes."

"Mister, that is the easiest hundred dollars I've ever earned," the attendant laughed, pocketing the bill. "There are no security cameras in the gym area. Plate glass windows are more than enough for the owner." He continued laughing.

"This hundred is for you and the other people not at the bench press. Talk to them quietly. Use the hundred and this second hundred to entertain them at the bar for the next fifteen minutes." Hull took out two more one-hundred-dollar bills, handing one to the attendant. "The second hundred is solely for you."

"I'll always be happy to take your money. What do I have to do to earn it?" The attendant reached for the second bill in Hull's hand.

"Clean up the mess I'm going to leave." Hull handed him the bill. "You've got ten minutes to convince the others to leave, thanks to the nice man at the counter. I'll wait here while you persuade them."

Hull stood at the desk, seemingly reading a bodybuilding magazine. The attendant, showing the few others in the gym their drinking money, had little difficulty convincing them to join him at the adjoining bar.

Satisfied he was alone with the three men—still laughing loudly—Hull walked to the weight area and selected two fifty-pound dumbbells, one for each hand. Walking slowly with his arms at his sides, he approached the bench press area.

The three men were standing. The largest of the three had his back to Hull, while the other two noticed Hull standing directly behind him. There could be no mistake—the larger man had a tattoo of an ape on the bicep of his left arm. Alerted by the others, the large man turned to face Hull. He was an inch or two shorter, with a muscular physique that gave him an air of power and intimidation.

"You're standing too close to me. This bench is being used. Now leave, or I'll be forced to injure you," he said, laughing, as were the other two.

"I'll only leave," Hull said, "if 'Ape'—the name your friends called out while you were beating a man with bullet wounds—wants me to. Did that make you feel like you accomplished something worth celebrating?"

"You're beginning to annoy me. What I do is none of your concern. If I did what you claim, why am I not in jail?" He stepped closer, expecting to throw a punch at the man standing toe-to-toe with him.

Hull stepped in closer still, making it impossible for the other man to gain leverage. "The defenseless man you enjoyed punishing is an exceptionally good friend of mine. He's currently fighting for his life. I want to give you something to remember him by."

Whether by anger or instinct, Hull slammed the fifty-pound dumbbells into each side of "Ape's" head. The other two men stood there, mouths and eyes wide open. Their friend's head morphed to half its original width and twice the length, resembling an under-inflated football. Blood and bone erupted from Ape's skull. Fragments of bone pierced his brain, killing him instantly.

Hull shoved the dead body toward the other two.

"Tell me the name of the person who sent you to kill the two FBI agents," he demanded.

One of the two stopped laughing, reaching for the revolver tucked into the small of his back. It was too little, too late. Hull's sword appeared out of nowhere, slicing the man's jugular vein and spewing blood into the face of the remaining man.

"I'll give you ten seconds to tell me the name of the person who issued the orders." Hull held his blade millimeters from the man's eyes.

"If I tell you, he'll have me killed," the man said in a squeaky voice, now covered in tears.

The blade struck bone in the man's left hand, separating his thumb from the rest of it. The man went into shock, screaming, "The only name I know is *Mischa*!"

Hull cleaned his blade, turned, and walked toward the exit, leaving another hundred-dollar bill on the attendant's table.

24

Team Must relocate

CIA Training room

Langley Virginia

March 28 0700 Hours

Your Russian computer hacker is safely stationed in another room, guarded by two Marines, Ashley said, laughing. "He claims he's never heard of you, but being free from hell in Russia, he didn't care who you were."

"John, it's true I never met Willi. My first choice was a friend of mine, Gregor, who has truly remarkable and unique computer skills. When I contacted him, he told me a hit-and-run driver crashed into his motorcycle in Moscow. Fortunately, he managed to avoid a total impact by angling the cycle. He suffered a broken leg and numerous bodily injuries, making travel impossible. He recommended Willi as his technical accomplice in recent illegal transactions. Very smart, with very little regard for the law—that's how Willi was described to me. I'll meet with him later."

Hull shifted tone. "John, I'm convinced the attack on your vehicle, Peters and Blake being shot, combined with the attack on Jaz, Donna, and my wife, was the result of one or more moles planted inside the White House. You need to start serious surveillance of recent hires there. Whoever hired them has money, high-level technical skills, and a mercenary army at their disposal."

Hull returned to reviewing his notes. "I'm traveling to Hollywood tonight to meet with the Red Cell team early tomorrow. You'll be needed to keep my team undercover while I'm away."

"Not to change the subject," Ashley said, "but were you near the Belgrade Fortress in downtown D.C. last night?" He continued, "The D.C. police have a high-speed data link to the White House security team. Anything unusual is tracked in real time and added to our database to anticipate threats of any kind. The police reported a string of deaths at a local gym. One man had his throat severed ear to ear; another bled to death after losing his thumb. A third had his head compressed as if a massive vise crushed it. Just letting you know—if anyone asks, you were with me until after midnight last night." Ashley smiled, searching Hull's stoic expression for clues.

"John, did you send your family to a safer site?" Hull asked. "I made plans last night to move mine to a secure location. You're welcome to join us, if the President thinks it's wise."

"My team, except for Blake, is due here in fifteen minutes—just enough time to make myself another cup of coffee. Want one?"

"Normally, I'd say yes, but my stomach lining's not ready for what you consider coffee," John laughed.

***

"As you all know, there were several attempts to injure or kill members of our team yesterday," Hull stated emphatically at the morning meeting. "Our team is clearly viewed as a serious threat by unknown enemies. Last night, I took steps to shield us from public view. Your laptops, phones, watches—anything remotely connected to the internet—must be placed in this lead-lined container by the end of the day. Change all passwords on your bank accounts, stock trading accounts, and social media. Replacements for internet access will be provided at our new base. The level of technical expertise targeting us exceeds any known threats faced by the FBI or CIA."

"Why do we have to move? I was just getting comfortable here," Jaz said, deadpan.

"Because I want to keep all of you alive," Hull replied directly. "Your picture was enough to trace your phone number and GPS. Peters and Blake's exact locations were known to their attackers. Same for Jaz and Donna, who were followed into the restaurant by their now-dead shadows. Willi, our new teammate, will investigate who is targeting us."

"Our glorious leader will be basking in the Hollywood sun tomorrow," Ashley added, "while the rest of you are transported at 0400 hours in a military convoy headed for Andrews Air Force

Base." He could sense their dismay at the early departure time. Stifling a smile, he continued, "I have to meet with the President at 1000 hours to initiate details for a bidder's conference early next week. Much as I'd like to join you, my hands are tied. MadMan will provide packing instructions."

Just then, Marine guards carrying automatic weapons opened the doors.

"As of now, you must travel in pairs with an armed escort," Ashley continued. "Jaz, John, Chasey, and MadMan are your escorts. Donna is returning to Johns Hopkins. Blake requires constant medical care. The FBI has taken over guard duty for Blake and Donna. Tamara and Peters—when she returns—will also need protection."

***

Office of Allen Parris

Alpha Technologies

1230 Hours

Speaking on his Genius cell phone, Parris grinned at Novak's description of how his main funding obstacle had "mysteriously" passed away.

"Let me repeat—you want me to give Hickler another million euros. I understand no one else could've accomplished what she did."

Before he could hang up, his secretary opened the door halfway to announce a pizza delivery. Allen looked confused—he hadn't ordered pizza.

Brushing her aside stepped a short, burly man with heavily tattooed arms. He extended his hand.

"We've never been properly introduced. My name is Mischa. We've done a lot of business by phone, but never met in person."

Parris recognized the name but was stunned by Mischa's presence. Their agreement had always been: no face-to-face contact.

"Your assignments yesterday cost me a great deal of money. I came to renegotiate our verbal contract," Mischa said, pounding the desk for emphasis.

"Wait, I don't understand," Parris replied, his voice rising to match Mischa's. "Ashley's car was destroyed. Do you want a bonus?"

"Sadly, the TV commentator assumed Ashley was in the car— he wasn't. He's alive," Mischa said, breathing heavily through his mouth. "Three women were targeted during lunch. I gave orders to eliminate all of them. None were touched, to my knowledge. And I haven't heard from my men. That can only mean one thing—they're either dead or have vanished. Other members of my staff are searching for them."

He continued, "Intercepting the FBI agents was easier thanks to the GPS locations you provided. Shooting them in the back was accomplished quickly. One of my men, Ape, wanted to earn the blood bonus you offered. He kept striking the wounded agent until a third agent started firing as he ran toward them."

Now nearly gasping, Mischa pulled a photo from an envelope and shoved it under Parris's eyes.

"I came to show you this picture taken on the gym manager's phone. Can you identify him?"

Parris studied the image. "I've never seen this man. The photo only shows one side of his face. Maybe I can enhance it with more time. Why are you showing me this?"

"That man destroyed three of my best people last night. Ape— the same one who beat the FBI agent—had his head smashed like a grape. Another had his throat slit so deep it nearly decapitated him. The third bled out after losing his thumb and part of his hand. You and I should both want to identify this man. Yesterday cost me five good men. I'm charging you one million per man. I expect a check before I leave. Any new assignments will be billed at one million dollars per person."

Parris swallowed hard. Mischa could tell he understood the gravity of the situation—just by watching his pupils dilate.

"Wait here. I'll go to accounting for your check. It'll say 'transportation services for large-scale testing platforms,'" Allen said quickly as he left the office.

Check in hand, Mischa showed no grief for his fallen men. His only thought, as he drove away, was how to recruit replacements with better skills and more advanced training.

***

CIA building

Technical Resource Room 4A

1700 Hours

Gazing at the note Ashley had given him, Hull opened the door, waving the two bored Marine guards away after showing them his credentials.

Willi's head never turned from his computer screen as Hull entered. Two slices of pizza remained in the oil-soaked box.

"I see my Russian friend has educated you on what great pizza tastes like," Hull said. His voice made Willi aware of another presence in the room.

"You must be Roy Hull—the man who travels in silence and kills the same way," Willi said, laughing as he raised his head. "Gregor told me all about you and how you operate. During my forced confinement, I've gained a lot of background on you. Don't let me ruin the surprise your wife has planned for you, you lucky man. One other thing: your personal taxes haven't been filed by your accounting staff. They're waiting for the payment receipt from a rental vehicle you purchased last year in Oklahoma."

Gregor's assessment was now verified beyond doubt. The facts quoted by Willi were not readily available. Hull's personal accountant resided in Eagles Bluff, Montana. The vehicle he had purchased in Oklahoma was bought using secret drug money—known only to him and the car agency.

"Turn your computer off. I need to speak with you," Hull said in a voice that left no room for argument. "Soon, you'll join the rest of my team. Yesterday, several members were placed in extreme danger. Their movements were tracked by an internet genius. All of their internet connectivity has now been disabled. Your job here is to build firewalls, along with spyware, to block all future threats—and, if possible, identify the organization tracking them."

"How do I refer to you? Boss or Hull?" Willi asked, framing the innocent question with genuine curiosity.

"Call me Hull. What else do you know about me?"

"Only what Gregor told me while we were working together in prison. You're one of his best friends. He also said you know all the laws—and how to break them when it fits your mission." Willi turned toward Hull and laughed. "That's my motto, too."

"Your life could be in danger if the people you're blocking find out your identity and location. Fortunately for you, several of your teammates are highly skilled combat professionals. After tonight, you do not venture outside the area I've secured without one or two of those professionals. Do you understand?"

Hull waved to the two Marines guarding the doorway.

"Take him to the others. MadMan Diana is in charge and knows what is necessary."

25

Hull Meets with Red Cell

Los Angeles, California

CIA Building Room 506

Senior Agent Brent Miluer greeted Hull at the doorway. "I trust you had a pleasant flight, Mr. Hull. Glancing at the visitor's name tag, I see from my checklist you called this meeting. The Red Cell individuals you named are seated in the conference room. Coffee and sweet rolls are a staple for all Red Cell meetings.

"If I can be frank, how did you know the composition of individuals in our local Red Cell unit? We never advertise or mention their existence to the outside world. Before you enter, permit me to give you a summary of the people attending. Your guests include two senior motion picture executives, one senior union screenwriter executive, a key grip and gaffer team—and one dressed as an alien—two Middle Eastern terrorists (nice young men from UCLA), a cowboy, two African-American men dressed in native costumes, and one white dude dressed as a cowboy."

"Easy enough to answer," Hull grinned. "There was a situation last year that required my skill set in military operations in a foreign nation. My specific knowledge of the geography and customs of that country led the head of Red Cell to requisition the former President to involve me. Being a shadow organization has its benefits.

"The producers, directors, writers, actors and actresses, and the stunt personnel form a highly complex and efficient operation. 9/11 was a wake-up call to the nation's intelligence agencies. It was explained to me that, before that day, large commercial jets crashing into towering office buildings were never considered a possibility by any of this country's intelligence services.

"When the impossible happened, the collective thought within the government was that preventing attacks before they happened was a more advantageous policy. Who better to conjure up disasters than the people who get paid to think of the unthinkable?"

"Unfortunately, all too accurate," Agent Miluer responded. "I see your guests are anxious to begin. I'll check in with you later with lunch and dinner menus." Miluer shook Hull's hand. "Good luck today."

Striding briskly to the lectern placed strategically in front of the assembled Red Cell team, Hull began:

"My name is Roy Hull. You have been asked to assist me in learning more about a strange terror confronting our country."

Waving a copy of the "Top Secret" report in front of him, Hull spoke in his usual deep baritone voice.

"Each of you has been given a *Top Secret* copy outlining the reasons and potential dangers confronting our country. Our mission today is basic intelligence work combined with massive uncertainty. Help me find a solution. I promise to end any and all dangers facing our country."

Hull waved the report again and sat down.

"Yes, we had an opportunity to discuss it among our group," the producer and director, Joseph Kuenzli, said loud enough for all to hear. "It would help our understanding if you could shed some light on how people can suffocate, as the material suggests, in broad daylight in outdoor conditions. The delivery system, as we see it, is narrowed down to one of two options.

"William Kravit, our technical adviser, suggested either a stealth drone or fleet of drones controlled by operators near the victims, or a satellite governed by an outside enemy entity—armed with some type of device that can cause suffocation in open environments."

"Exactly my thoughts," Hull said, "which is the reason I've selected the most competent and methodical medical person I know. The doctor's name is known only to my team for security reasons. We have never been able to examine the victims in a timely fashion. The President and his Chief of Staff have placed every resource I require at my disposal to find out what and how—in a more timely manner—should future tragedies strike."

Hull's voice was strong and confident. He wasn't certain if it convinced the group of exceptionally talented media personnel.

"I have a question nobody has raised," said Kathy Walker, head of the scriptwriters union. "All conversations up to this point have centered on the method of death. When I read your notes, my first question was: *why*?

"Who benefits from the deaths of average citizens in three different countries? If I were to write a storyline, that would be my opening scene. From my perspective, finding the people who benefit the most would lead to the same people responsible for the bizarre deaths."

Hull's mind flashed to the attempted murders of his own team. There had to be a connection—he was certain of that fact. Walker's comments pushed him to respond.

"For once, I am speechless," Hull said, rising from his seat. "Yesterday, I failed to mention—my team was attacked on three different occasions. Until Kathy voiced her concerns, I hadn't tied economic advantages to my thought process. This introduces a totally new approach—to both mine and your thinking. Would someone care to expand on Kathy's remarks?"

"A group of us found it strange no ransom letters were sent to the countries mentioned in your notes. Killing people for the sake of killing is not a profitable enterprise," said Jack Dagnon, a leading actor in many action military movies.

"I agree with Jack's thinking," added Sue Amt, a senior motion picture financial adviser, "not only because I want him to star in my next production, but realistically, what he says is true—killing for the sake of killing is only rational if you want to take over control of that country. From your notes, controlling the country doesn't make sense."

Jerome Siegel, head of Epic Picture Corporation, stood up and looked directly at Hull. "An old movie standard: if you follow the money, everything else will fall into place."

"If you'll forgive me," Hull said, "I need to expedite my return. Your insights are causing me to rethink how to deploy my resources. Sorry to leave with such short notice. Time is now more precious than ever.

"Thank you, one and all, for giving me your time and thoughts."

Hull rose and asked Agent Miluer to arrange lunch for his guests as he raced down the hallway.

26

Parris Stalled

Alpha Technologies

MAX Parris executive office

0700 Hours

Another Ashley delaying tactic to stall the flow of millions of dollars to his company. Max Parris knew how devious Ashley could be, hiding behind the bureaucratic stonewall. Announcing a bidder's conference for early next week would create a month-long delay in reaching the inevitable decision of awarding the contract to his company.

Leafing through the list of responding companies, he mentally eliminated most of his peers automatically. They did not have the intellectual, scientific, and mathematical cadre of employees to be considered. This threat created a national need for a highly technical workforce, which he had assembled over the past months. Knowing the threat facing the country was the first stage in gaining unprecedented wealth.

Max smiled. Since only he and two others could predict where and when a calamity would strike, he and his friends would position their solution at a designated location—knowing nothing would strike the space they guarded.

Parris concluded that companies responding consisted mainly of technical firms residing in the D.C. area or adjacent suburbs. One new company caught his attention: Hull Technologies, based in Montana, had never responded to a Department of Defense weapons conference before. Searching for basic information on the company alerted Max that they were the leading supplier of software controlling Liquid Distribution, used to minimize wastage of precious fuel consumed by planes and vehicles.

The president, he noted, was a graduate of the Naval Academy, which was a plus in government defense spending. More bad news: the leading sales executive for the firm was a retired naval admiral who had served as commandant at the U.S. Naval Academy. Strangely still, both had the same last name—Ungle. Nothing that a few well-placed bribes couldn't overcome.

He was ready to close the website when the picture of the founder and CEO of Hull Technologies flashed on the screen. The name meant nothing. But the picture of Roy Hull sent a cold shiver down his spine. Hull's picture and the photo Mischa had left him were one and the same. Much more digging was necessary, Max pondered—but this could not be good.

After several hours of legal and illegal computer searches that uncovered little, Parris jotted down several pages of notes:

First in his class at the Naval Academy. Former SEAL. Marine Recon. Medal of Honor awarded in 2002. Death of wife and small daughter in 2008. No record of military service two months after their death. Married a second time to Tamara Hull.

He jotted the name down on his smartphone.

Most of the detailed information he searched was heavily redacted—over half, if not more—causing Parris some distress. He picked up his phone and dialed a number used only for special fact-finding missions. Hull's complete information might cost him millions, but it was imperative he develop a full understanding of what Hull could or could not do to slow or stop the vast influx of dollars to the Parris treasury.

***

White House

John Ashley's Office

0900 Hours

Ashley returned from his daily briefing with the President. His ears were still ringing from the revelation that the country had paid a bribe to a Russian prison official. It was the only method available to secure Hull's "had-to-have" computer hacker.

His eye caught sight of an individual sitting across his desk. Startled, he relaxed when he recognized Roy Hull—sitting with a big smile on his face and an even bigger cup of coffee in his hand.

"You do know we have rules for entering my office?" Ashley laughed. "I should have you placed in handcuffs and thrown in jail. But from what I've heard, you'd be out of them before you hit the front door—leaving the two guards in a bad way."

Hull rose and shook Ashley's hand.

"The trip to California opened a completely new line of thinking for me—something that only you could recognize as a possible reason to murder innocent civilians. In the meeting, the question was raised: *Who will benefit most from the unknown terror threat?* You have a more analytical background in this area. What can you share with me on companies or individuals positioned to benefit the most?"

Hull finished his coffee, waiting for Ashley to respond.

"Those actions would indicate a diseased mind," Ashley replied. "However, I could list three to four companies headed by individuals who wouldn't be above creating a crisis for personal gain. Let me do some thinking and get back to you."

He paused, then continued. "Before you left, you wanted all the information I could gather on a man named Mischa." Ashley searched his desk and pulled out a folder. "This file contains all of the details the D.C. police and FBI collected on him. I can summarize: high-level crime chief employing mostly Eastern European criminals. Involved in murder, theft, and extortion. Skillfully hides his participation by using recruited members to carry out his role in any criminal activities. He boasts that law enforcement will never be able to find him guilty."

"Is my team headquartered at Andrews?" Hull asked. "My new Russian friend now becomes more important to our joint effort. Mischa no doubt ordered the attacks on my team. How or when we meet—only one of us will survive."

Ashley had never seen that threatening look in Hull's eyes before.

"Before you leave," Ashley said hesitantly, "the President asked me a question I found difficult to believe. He mentioned in his conversations with Doctor Donna Running Deer that she disclosed your blood type is unknown to science. You have a mixture of human and reptilian blood. To survive, should you be injured, this unlikely combination must be transfused."

He chuckled uncomfortably. "I laughed out loud, thinking the President was playing a practical joke on me. But he emphasized— more than once—that I ask you about it. Sorry, I laughed so hard; my position with him might be in jeopardy."

Ashley was still half-laughing when Hull responded in his usual matter-of-fact tone.

"He is very observant. The truth is stranger than fiction. When I was a noticeably young child, I was playing in a stream with Donna at Eagle Bluff, Montana. A large poisonous snake emerged from the water and bit me several times. I shouted out in pain. My body went limp. Donna carried me out of the water and ran to get my mother. She rushed me to the nearest hospital. After hours of treatment, my condition was deteriorating rapidly.

Knowing the local Native American healers had treated people with poisonous snake bites before, she asked that they be allowed to treat me. One of the doctors told my father they weren't going to argue with a woman waving a large revolver in front of them." Hull smiled. "My mother's version was not as dramatic."

"The Native American healer worked and prayed over me for the entire evening without taking a break. In the morning, my fever broke, and my pajamas were soaked as if I had gone swimming. Since that time, I need only a few hours of sleep per week. If I lose blood for any reason, I must replenish it with blood that Donna takes from my body at scheduled intervals. She keeps a supply with her at all times. My parents have a reserve, as do I—for emergencies."

Ashley stood dumbstruck.

"You are a very unusual individual, Hull," he finally said. "I'll give you that much."

Hull waved to him on his way out, leaving Ashley not fully understanding what he had just learned.

27

Hull Confers with Willi

Andrews Air Force Base

Prince George County, Maryland

April 23,

A blue-uniformed gate guard stopped Hull at the entrance. "Identification and destination, Mr. Hull," she said, glancing at his name tag as she wrote his name in the visitor log. "Your highly secured area is located two stops from the gate. Turn right at the second intersection. Mr. Ashley has left specific instructions for you and your team to receive our complete cooperation. Buildings A, B, and C are your destination."

Dan Chasey stood on the first step of Building A, speaking to a heavily bandaged FBI agent.

"Are those bandages for support or sympathy?" Chasey asked, dodging a fake punch Peters aimed at his head.

"The hospital only released me on the condition I protected my wounds. Look, Mister Smart Ass—if you'd been a little faster, I wouldn't be injured at all." Peters grinned, faking another blow to Chasey's face.

"Hold on," Hull laughed. "I can't have two of my team fighting each other. Walk inside with me and bring me up to date."

"MadMan has the team training on the new DDM4 V7 assault rifle you chose," Chasey said as they walked. "Peters and I took an early practice session. I found its accuracy at five hundred yards much better than any rifle I've used in the past."

"I appreciated the weight and ease of operation," Peters added. "If I have to carry it over a mile or more, it's easily the best weapon I've ever used."

"Where's Willi's work area? I may need you two to assist him in using your sources on selected individuals. Red Cell members have opened up several new areas of potential criminal activity not previously considered. After I give Willi my new insights, I need to see my wife," Hull said, following his two team members.

"Before you see Willi, I need to give you some background on John Tsia," Chasey said. "He's pleasant enough and tends to keep to himself. MadMan asked him why he volunteered for this assignment. His commander—who you know—told him you wanted his best soldier, someone with deep-diving experience." Chasey paused, waiting for a response.

"Last night, after settling in, the team gathered in the rec room to get a better understanding of our individual and combined strengths and weaknesses. Yes, everyone had their favorite liquid refreshment—including your wife, who, I might add, has the liquid capacity of a camel."

Hull laughed aloud. "I bet she was drinking Stolie—Stolichnaya vodka—neat. It's a trait she picked up from my father."

"Sorry, I interrupted your story."

"Most of us are military, ex-military, or law enforcement. After a few drinks, someone raised the question of our personal favorite weapons for close combat. I started by drawing my standard-issue SEAL SRK from my custom sheath. Jaz showed us her Spetsnaz knife concealed in her ankle holster—the same one she used to defend Donna, Tamara, and herself during the attack.

"MadMan proudly extracted his Green Beret 'Yarborough' knife from his boot sheath. Tamara told us that after France, you ordered her to always carry her .357 snub-nosed hammerless revolver."

Chasey mimicked her action. "She reached behind and flashed it in front of us. We laughed when she said, 'Not silent, but very effective.'"

"Don't laugh," Hull said seriously. "She killed three men in Montana defending my father, and two in Florida who were trying to take her life. She's not a SEAL or Special Forces equal, but she's certainly efficient. She sometimes joins me for self-defense training when time permits."

"All well and good," Chasey nodded. "Now, back to John's close-combat weapon of choice. I, like the rest of us, was unprepared for what he showed us.

"After everyone else had gone, John rose from his chair and asked the people on the far side of the table to move over to his side. He scanned for a suitable target, picked up a thick book, placed it on the bar ledge, and returned to his spot. We had no idea what he was doing.

"In a flash, he reached into a small bag on his hip. Flashes of black and silver flew across our field of vision. I counted five—maybe six—objects. It couldn't have taken more than three seconds. John retrieved the book and held it up for us.

"Six small spheres with razor-sharp edges had sliced halfway through it. 'Good from one to ten meters,' he said. 'Silent, shocking, and deadly—my weapon for close-interval battles.' We just sat there, dumbfounded."

"He was showing you there are many ways to disable or kill an enemy. Most people call them 'shooting stars,' but their technical name is *shuriken*—throwing weapons," Hull said, smiling a bit wider as he recalled his training. "Did he show you the different shapes he uses? I haven't used them since my early training days at the Sheisin school in Japan."

Peters laughed. "We begged John to teach us. We all tried and failed miserably to throw them right. Your wife, though—she became obsessed with learning. After we left, she stayed behind for more training. This morning at breakfast, she showed me a shooting star attached to her bracelet. John told her to wear it since she might never throw it properly—but if attacked, it could still be useful."

Laughing, Hull replied, "Another reason to stay on her good side. I take it John has erased any doubt about his fighting ability. Now take me to Willi—he's pivotal in identifying who and where our enemies are."

***

Room 3A

Building C

1100 Hours

Willi needed some exercise. His body ached from travel and the too-soft mattress in his room. If only he could find a bicycle to ride—he'd bring it up with the head man when the time was right.

He typed in a command, not sure exactly what he was searching for. Agent Peters had explained why he was part of the team—his skill set might be the only way to uncover the multi-pronged threats facing the three countries.

He gathered the known data points from the various attacks and printed them out for the others. Immersed in search queries and cross-referencing, he was deep in concentration when the door opened.

"Willi, I see you've adapted to your new home quite well," Hull said, entering. "I spoke to Dr. Deer during my return from California. She told me you two worked for hours narrowing down the time and location of the death attacks." Hull shook Willi's hand as he spoke.

Willi laughed. "I speak poor English, and the good doctor knows only a few Russian phrases. If this situation weren't so vital, our 'conversation' would have made a hilarious comedy skit. She is very bright, though, and interpreted the information I needed to present a clearer analysis of why people are dying of strangulation without visible marks.

"The same applies to the animals that died. Dr. Deer contacted her medical colleagues in Russia and China, sharing information on the deceased. Her research into body temperature and lividity was our starting point.

"After dinner last night, we came to several tentative conclusions, which I printed out for you and the team." He handed the documents to Hull. "Our summary shows the attacks occurred at different times in each country—first in Russia, then one to two hours later in China, with an eight-hour gap before attacks were reported in your country."

Hull took a moment to absorb the information. "You're as good as my friend Gregor said. In the future, if it helps, we can speak in your native language. My meetings in California suggest these horrible deaths might be more about money than power. I need your help identifying individuals who stand to gain from supplying defense systems against these unknown, deadly threats.

"If you need support, Agent Peters—the one with the bandages around her head—will assist you." Hull stood and shook Willi's hand.

"Can you help me find a bicycle?" Willi asked. "I can jog with the others, but I prefer riding, especially with such beautiful scenery. I heard there are several trails on base."

"Rest assured," Hull smiled. "Find the bike you want, and it's yours."

Chasey and Peters left with Hull.

"Now, I'm more than anxious to see my wife," Hull said with emphasis.

"Well, you'll have to wait," Peters replied. "I saw her drive off a few minutes before you pulled up. We reminded her she needed an escort, but she just waved us off. She left some folders at the CIA building that she needed. Told us not to worry—she'd be back within two hours."

28

Max Parris Contacts Hickler

Alpha Technologies Building

Office of Max Parris

April 29, 0500 Hours

Max was extremely pleased. His secret, very expensive operative had become a trusted member of the senior staff in John Ashley's department. The agent had delivered the information in person at 0400 hours. When making highly critical decisions, his rule was that having the most current information was a necessity.

Opening his ever-present laptop, Max studied each element in detail. Much of the information included in his agent's report he had read previously while making notes on his laptop. More "Eyes Only" details caused some uneasiness in his mind.

A partial explanation of Hull's disappearance from military duty upon resignation was set forth in a Presidential directive dated 2008. It appointed Hull to the President's and nation's "Wet Work," including murders and assassinations, without being an agent of the government. Each assignment would come directly from the Executive Office through a third-party interface known to Hull. The last line in the directive clearly stated that if caught and convicted in the United States or its allies, Hull was to secretly be released without punishment.

Max digested additional material enclosed in a separate document. This material was even more interesting. Hull spoke and read twelve or more languages fluently and was reported to speak a dozen more, including Eastern and Middle Eastern languages. Most troubling was Hull's martial arts training. He had earned his tenth-degree black belt designation at the age of sixteen. The code name given to him by his sensei was "Instant Death," which the author described as most appropriate given his range of skills. The psychological report on Hull labeled him a borderline psychopath who made and played by his own unique definition of right and wrong.

Max stopped, thinking to himself. *No wonder Mischa's men met their swift and painful death. They had upset a man with unlimited physical abilities and no conscience.*

The report included several pictures he had seen before. A few caught his interest—particularly the ones with Hull and a beautiful woman who stood only a few inches shorter than Hull, with long, flaming red hair. Her name was Tamara Reed Hull. Max instantly recognized Tamara Reed as the owner and CEO of the hedge fund Reed Worldwide Investments, specializing in serving women's financial needs throughout the world. Another article described the recent merger of World Wide with another hedge fund owned and managed by one Patrice Hull.

Tamara Hull had never registered in Max's mind before, but he now understood two things. The first was that Mischa had mentioned his agents in the restaurant told him there were three women having lunch. They could only identify two from the pictures they were given. The third woman was Tamara Hull, no doubt. Tamara was Hull's most vulnerable weakness. Max was already plotting how to use it for maximum advantage.

He placed a call to Mischa. Although early, it made no difference to him. Leaving a detailed voicemail message, he turned to his computer, sending a variety of pictures to Mischa. A detailed note accompanied both pictures. The message for Hull's note was simple:

Under no circumstances—repeat, none—do not engage in physical combat. Your staff is not adequate to engage.

Max's instructions regarding Tamara were more detailed:

I believe from my sources Hull's team is staying at Andrews Air Force Base. The woman's name is Tamara Hull. I need her captured. Torture for information is allowed, but she must be kept alive. Tamara is my most valuable future bargaining chip. She is easily identified. She drives a bright red Chevrolet Corvette with a white top. Her company's logo is painted on the hood. You will require multiple vehicles to chase and capture her. The engine in the car, I am informed, has even been modified to produce speeds only racing cars can reach.

Parris took his special cell phone from his pocket. He knew the call was secure, even though the party he was calling did not have a similar phone. Dialing Argentina's international number, he waited for a response from an answering service. He had used this technique in the past.

"Yes, please leave a message for Fraulein Hickler. I will meet her tomorrow at 1600 hours. Book a private room for dinner. I arrive on my corporate jet by 1500 hours. Arrange transportation for me."

If any person or group could defeat Hull, Hickler and her team had superior talent and training to others in the same profession.

29

Tamara Defies Orders

Andrews Air Force Base

Living quarters of Tamara and Roy Hull

I know the Stash folder is here somewhere, Tamara laughed at herself. Packing up from the first motel close to CIA headquarters had to be accomplished in an extremely limited timeframe. Yet she was certain all of her files had been checked, loaded, and transported safely to the Andrews facility.

It suddenly dawned on her that the file was sitting by the phone in her old apartment. She had needed the information from it while discussing details of their proposal with her partner—Patrice Hull, the mother of her husband.

Glancing at her watch, her decision was made. Hopefully, her husband would not return for another hour from California.

Throwing on a pair of jeans and a long-sleeve U.S. Navy T-shirt—compliments of her husband's wardrobe—she laced on her favorite pair of running shoes. She placed the bracelet with the shooting star on her right wrist. Her final clothing selection was the holster with her hammerless .357 Magnum. It felt like it had always been tucked into her lower back.

Picking up the phone, she called the motel.

"Hello, this is Tamara Hull. Last week, I stayed in apartment 23A. Did, by chance, your cleaning staff find and turn in a green folder with my initials, T.H., on the front of it? Great, keep it at the front desk. You and your staff will be rewarded well."

Tamara was going to ignore her husband's strict orders that all team members travel with a companion.

I can be back before anyone notices I left.

***

Dan Chasey and MadMan Diana recognized Tamara's one-of-a-kind Corvette as it sped to the exit gate.

"Where is she going? You can tell Roy when he returns," MadMan laughed. He knew from experience—Hull had a really short fuse when someone disobeyed a direct order, even if she was married to him.

***

Emily Heger knew exactly what she had to do. Mischa paid her well for CIA information.

"Mischa, a Tamara Hull is coming to the motel in thirty minutes or so. She left a file in her room, which is in my possession. Your orders were to notify you if any of our guests from last week made a return appearance. You have always been most generous in paying me. Is there a bonus for this information? Thank you. Have your men report to me. I will do whatever they ask."

***

Bumper-to-bumper traffic was a constant when leaving the base. After a few miles, the highway showed signs of open pavement—just what Tamara was hoping for. Eying little traffic in the outside lane, she pressed gently on the accelerator. She knew the instantaneous speed was the sole reason she had paid an exorbitant amount for this car.

Nothing interesting was visible in her rearview mirror. More than once, her vigilance had saved her from a speeding ticket. Checking one more time, a large black sedan began to appear, edging closer to her.

Tamara began to feel guilty for not following her husband's strict partner rule when traveling outside the base. To ease her conscience, a quick call to his private cell would make her feel better—especially if it went directly to voicemail.

"Roy, this is Tam. I didn't pack an important T.H. folder. Yes, the very same color you—what did you name it—*gauche*? How can anyone, especially me, miss my Kelly green–colored folder? Heading to the apartment we stayed at last week. Desk staff person, Emily, told me she had it and would hold it for me. Love you. See you when you return."

Checking her speed, Tamara couldn't help but notice a light green panel truck had now replaced the black sedan in her rearview mirror.

Still twenty minutes from her destination, her mind began to review the key points in their proposal. Turning onto the access road to the motel, Tamara became slightly concerned when the black sedan *and* the green panel truck turned into the same exit.

The message her husband lived by echoed in her mind: *"If you think there is trouble, there is."*

Tamara pushed the single key for Roy Hull on her cell.

"Roy, this may be nothing, but I think people are following me. I am turning into the motel parking lot."

Tamara locked her car just as the black sedan and green panel truck entered the parking lot. Coincidence or not, her best chance for security would be inside the motel. Her footsteps moved faster toward the motel's entrance, driven by an unknown fear.

30

Tamara Captured

Motel Parking lot

April

0900 Hours

Tamara glanced back at the two cars she believed had followed her, relieved to see two men speaking and smoking in front of their vehicles. Smiling inwardly—just being around her husband had heightened her danger signals.

No reason to worry, she thought—when a pair of unseen, very muscular arms wrapped her in a deadly embrace that quickly disrupted her thinking.

The attacker, as planned, had been waiting for Tamara to be distracted by the two men. His arms muffled any sound struggling to escape from her body. He began to choke the breath out of her, aiming to render her unconscious.

The primal, animal instincts buried in the far reaches of her brain kicked into overdrive. Roy had instructed her repeatedly on the major defensive measures to use when attacked from behind, constantly drilling:

"Jerk your head back violently, trying to strike the attacker in the face or neck to loosen the grip. Next, take your right foot and crunch into the instep of the attacker."

Roy had made her practice these moves on him countless times. Without a second thought, Tamara went into defensive mode. She could tell her attacker wasn't expecting this response.

He threw her to the ground, ready to subdue and inflict pain on this woman. Tamara rolled across the pavement as Roy had trained her, reaching instinctively for her revolver. She could sense—and then see—blood streaming from the attacker's nose.

Screaming that he was going to hurt and humiliate her, he hurled himself onto Tamara's body. The hammerless .357 punched a hole where his right eye had been. Tamara shoved his body away and stood up.

She recalled Roy's instruction:

"One shot is good; two is better."

Following protocol, the second round completely displaced the left side of his head.

Holstering her weapon, Tamara's head was suddenly and unexpectedly filled with darkness.

***

"Take one arm. The chemicals we used to subdue her will only last thirty minutes. Emily gave me a key to the motel's laundry room. Once we have her secured, I'll contact Mischa. He didn't warn us this woman was armed and dangerous. Emily's staff can erase any presence of our dead friend—no problem. We owe that bitch some punishment when she wakes up."

***

Andrews Air Force Base

Willi's Room

1100 Hours

Hull turned to Chasey and MadMan. "Which rooms are Tam and I staying in?"

Chasey turned to MadMan. "I'll let you handle this one."

Taking a deep breath to collect his thoughts, MadMan turned to face Roy Hull. "We can show you the rooms assigned to you and your wife. However, the bad news is... you won't find Tam there. Dan and I saw her drive off about thirty minutes before you arrived at the front gate. She and her fire engine red Corvette were fast out of the compound. We raised our arms to signal her to stop, but she just waved and exited into traffic."

MadMan was at a loss for what to say next.

Roy Hull, who always practiced self-control over his emotions, now had a face flushed with frustration.

"Did I not make it *crystal clear* to everyone—no person is to leave this base without an armed escort? Why did you two not escort her?"

"Roy, she never indicated she was leaving the base and never asked either of us to join her. Where she's headed, we have no clue. As I said, we waved our arms to stop her, but she plainly ignored us," Chasey replied, clearly irritated by Hull's anger at both him and MadMan.

"Forgive me," Hull said quickly. "The lessons I gained from the Red Cell meeting are causing me to rethink our enemies. It's apparent that major international organizations have combined forces. What puzzles me is what, why, and how many are involved. Until we know that, every person we come in contact with is a suspected enemy. Tam leaving without notice and protection just adds to my list of anxieties."

Hull's private phone vibrated, signaling a voicemail message. Holding it close to his ear, he listened to his wife's comical, typical Tamara-style explanation for her rapid departure without an escort. She detailed that she was driving to the motel where they had stayed last week and mentioned Emily and her colorful green folder. She promised to be back within the hour.

Patience was not one of Hull's virtues.

He dialed Tamara's phone. No answer.

Strange, he thought. Dialed again—voicemail.

"Time has passed for Tamara's return. I need to go to the motel we stayed at last week. Tamara's life might be at stake," he cried out in anguish.

"Come with me!" MadMan shouted. "I have the fastest way for you to get there. Ashley provided us with an entire fleet of aircraft. There's a copter that can bypass traffic. I can set it down in the parking lot or any other vacant location you desire. Chase, you want to join us?"

"Sure. Was there any doubt?" Chasey laughed, following Hull and MadMan to the holding area for Hull's private Air Force.

31

Max meets Hickler

Max Meets Hickler

Bahia Blanca Argentina

Headquarters of Kim Hickler

April 1100 Hours

How was your journey, Max? I was pleasantly surprised when you phoned me last week requesting a face-to-face meeting. You are the only member of your group I have had the honor of meeting in this manner. Quite unusual, no?

Kim Hickler's youthful face, framed by long black hair, masked her reputation as one of the world's most accomplished assassins. She was well-known among those seeking to eliminate competitors, witnesses, and law enforcement officials. When all others fail, call me for guaranteed results.

"You have something for me, Max?" Kim smiled, holding out her hand.

Max had to admit, walking down the long, narrow hallway to Hickler's office was a rare treat. He observed a variety of plundered treasures—a Van Gogh painting, a Rubens statue, and other art from various eras. It was impressive. Kim Hickler was the ideal person to deal with Max's situation. She was brilliant and ruthless, two qualities he deeply admired.

Max Parris laughed. "A woman after my own heart. Yes, I have your cashier's check in this envelope. Novak sends his regards. But before I hand it over, we both want to know—how did you manage to eliminate his enemy so rapidly and skillfully when all others have failed?"

"First, hand me the check. Only then will I share one of my secrets."

Kim Hickler opened the envelope Max handed her. "Now, hand me that cane on the blue chair. Be careful—it has a recessed needle in the bottom cap. This is no ordinary cane. It contains a mixture of the most potent snake venom, combined with my own expertise. Once injected, a person has less than ten minutes to live. The beauty of it is that the poison mimics a heart attack."

She leaned forward, voice smooth and precise.

"I must confess, the marked person—Yuri—was heavily guarded by highly skilled professionals. Surprisingly, the woman in charge of managing the household took a nasty fall the week before I started. I, of course, using one of my aliases, was interviewed and hired as her replacement.

"One of my many duties was overseeing the wait staff delivering meals to the various dining areas. The main meal—supper—was always served in the formal dining room. Novak's enemy, Yuri, dined with a few friends every night. Their routine was that one of his friends would serve as a food taster. Poisoning is still quite common in Russia, so they were careful. Each course was tested before Yuri could begin eating, and the tasters always used different utensils than Yuri.

"The cane I had you hold was at my side. Clearly, I couldn't stab him in front of his guards, but I managed to place a few drops of venom from the cane on his knife and fork. The poison is extremely fast-acting. I left the dining room, gathered my belongings, and exited the home just as I heard his associates asking him what was wrong."

Parris was both amused and enthralled by the competent and deadly nature of Kim Hickler.

"The main reason I needed to see you in person," he said, "is because I have another high-value target who is troubling me. His name is Roy Hull."

Withdrawing a picture from his attaché case, Max selected Hull's photo from a file of ten. "I'll leave these pictures with you. He's many times more dangerous than Yuri. His résumé in combat is quite impressive. Once you've studied him, contact me with your fee. I need Hull eliminated—if my plan to kidnap his wife fails. I intend to use her as leverage to prevent him from interfering in the procurement of a billion-dollar defense system soon to be awarded to my company."

Hickler took the file, scanned it briefly, and placed it in a drawer, which she locked.

"Max, you traveled a long way. Let me show you how we produce your threats. First, you must understand the planning behind my team. In each country, we have established two independent networks.

"One team operates the flying machines, which are constantly undergoing technological upgrades. Those men and women travel here for training before each event you authorize. The second team is stationed near the target area. Their job is to prevent outsiders from investigating the dead bodies, maintaining secrecy regarding the cause of death. These operatives cost money—which you have paid.

"The next event you've commissioned is much larger in scope, necessitating the higher fees I've charged you. Everyone in my operation reports directly to me. The two men most vital to our success were eager to meet you. I announced the 'money man' was visiting us." Hickler laughed softly.

Parris followed her to the entrance, where a golf cart was waiting.

"Your town has something for everybody," Parris commented. "I see restaurants, cafés, and a fair number of nightclubs."

"Our people appreciate the finer things in life, Max. Unlike you and me—we favor wealth and power. I won't take you into either science laboratory, but we're very close to the site where deadly chemicals are produced. Kessler is a brilliant and practical scientist. His building is marked with a poison symbol to warn intruders.

"Everyone entering must wear protective clothing. Of course, unseen by the public, my armed guards ensure that no one goes where they shouldn't. Some curious people have disappeared without a trace."

Hickler drove the golf cart another five hundred yards, stopping in front of a large, spacious building with its doors open.

"You'll notice a large number of small aircraft being assembled. The next event you paid for—due to its scale—forced us to expand our manufacturing capabilities. I've been told your threats can be activated by early next week."

"Excellent on all points, Fräulein Hickler. It's a pleasure doing business with you and your associates. Now, if you'll be so kind as to drive me to my plane, I'm confident our combined efforts will bring us all very handsome returns."

Max was eager to inform his partners how quickly the threats would begin.

32

Green Folder

Motel Parking lot

April, 1100 Hours

Before MadMan could stop the blades from rotating, Hull was on the ground. The copter came to rest not more than two hundred yards from Tamara's fire-engine red Corvette.

"Dan, you and MadMan look for any sign of Tamara. Emily— the person Tam told me had her folder—is my first stop. I'll meet you by the copter in fifteen." Hull sprinted to the front door.

"Roy, stop! There are traces of blood not more than ten yards from the copter," MadMan shouted.

Roy Hull froze in his tracks. His heart and mind were racing. *Not again.* The memory of his first wife, Ashley, lying in her coffin—a victim of Iraqi terrorists in 2008—never left his consciousness. The attackers had mistaken Ashley for him, as his flight had been delayed. Ashley was driving his car, and the number of cruel and deadly slash marks inflicted on her body were too numerous to count.

Tamara, facing the same or worse fate, would cause him to lose all hope of sanity.

MadMan and Chasey examined the blood pooled in a half circle.

"The victim was dragged onto the grass. MadMan and I will follow the trail. Roy, it would be better for you to ask questions of the staff Tamara mentioned." Chasey didn't want Hull to discover his wife if she were fatally wounded.

"Right. If you discover anything, call me. The desk person—Emily—may have been the last person who spoke to Tam."

Hull half-ran into the motel entrance. His nerves were taut. Anything he could find—anything—would help relieve his tension. He couldn't see anyone in the lobby except a woman with long blonde hair standing behind the motel counter.

"Good morning. My name is Roy Hull. I believe my wife, Tamara, collected a folder from you this morning. She left me a message that 'Emily' had the folder at the front desk and was holding it for her." His voice was hesitant and strained.

"Yes, I was on duty and answered her phone call. My name is Emily, as you can read on my name tag. The woman you mentioned picked up a folder about thirty minutes ago. She was very pleasant and appreciative of my good work." Emily smiled at Hull.

"Did you notice which way she headed when she left?"

Hull was now starting to worry since Tamara hadn't contacted him after retrieving her money-green folder. He turned to leave when a flash of green, hidden under a pile of papers on Emily's desk, caught his attention. Hull instantly recognized the color of Tam's folders—and that Emily was lying.

With the speed of a striking snake, he grabbed Emily by her long blonde hair with both hands, dragged her across the counter, and threw her on the floor in front of him.

Emily cried out in pain. "Are you mad? My head is screaming in pain, you idiot!"

Hull kicked her violently in the rib cage.

"You will only enjoy more pain in the future. Stay motionless while I pick up my wife's folder."

Hull was in full combat mode—eyes narrowed to slits, breathing slowed to a tenth of a normal rate while his mind processed the facts. Tamara had never reached the motel lobby. She was either captured or dead—and he was determined to find her, no matter what it would take.

"On your feet. We're taking a trip to the parking area where my friends found some blood. I want answers."

Hull wrapped Emily's hair around his left hand, forcing her to stand as they marched to find MadMan and Chasey.

MadMan and Chasey stood with their mouths open at the sight of Hull dragging a woman with long blonde hair toward them.

"Did you have any luck tracking the person who was bleeding?" Hull asked, his voice carrying desperation.

"Our search ended at the parking lot. The bloody trail ended there. We both believe the person bleeding was taken away in a vehicle," MadMan said, knowing Hull did not want to hear those words.

Hull acted on instinct after hearing MadMan's description. Tightening his grip on Emily's scalp, he screamed into her face:

"What happened to my wife?"

Emily began to wail. "You'll never force that information from me. The man I work for will have me killed if I give you that information. No amount of pain will make me talk."

She was half crying, half laughing.

MadMan and Chasey had the identical thought: *Lady, you just said the wrong thing to Roy Hull.*

Her laughter ended abruptly when Hull pulled out his sword and severed her left ear from her scalp. Emily's knees started to buckle, not fully understanding what had just happened. She felt the pain— but the shock of seeing her ear on the ground overwhelmed her. Blood streamed down the side of her face.

"I'll give you five seconds before I take your right ear," Hull told her. "If your friends can bring more pain to bear on you than I can, I doubt you'll be alive much longer. Now—where is my wife? I have to know if she's dead or alive."

Chasey and MadMan held Emily under each arm to keep her from collapsing onto the ground. They had heard stories of Hull's savage nature—but neither had witnessed it firsthand. In their minds, they were asking the same question: *Was Hull sane—or insane?*

"Best you answer Mr. Hull's question about his wife," Dan Chasey said convincingly. "Or you'll end up in scraps in the parking lot. As you can see, he's in no mood to wait."

Emily's eyes grew wide as she continued to gaze at her severed ear on the pavement.

"She was taken by three men into the laundry building at the end of the complex, last I saw her. She's going to be punished for killing the brother of one of her attackers. They were instructed not to kill her, but any kind of punishment was allowed by our leader. In fact, she's such a valuable prize that Mischa is sending another vehicle with four men to take her to a more secure location."

She smirked through the pain.

"I may be dying, but I'm still better off than your wife once Mischa has her in his clutches."

Emily fainted from the pain—still laughing at Hull's dilemma.

***

Laundry Room

Motel

1230 Hours

"Tie her hands behind the chair. It will only be a few minutes before the drug wears off. Mischa wants her alive to be used as a hostage. His plan is to make sure her husband doesn't interfere in his wealthy friend's business operation. No need for a gag—this building is soundproof from all the laundry equipment. I have to phone Mischa to tell him where to pick up his prize. But first, when she's alert—notify me. I have a debt to collect for her killing my brother," Anton told the other two men before walking away.

Tamara's head was spinning. She ached from the top of her head to the soles of her feet. Worse, she could taste blood from where one of the men who drugged her had struck her multiple times. Her stomach was upset, and she was thirsty—but what really hurt was not listening to her husband's warnings.

"Can I get something to drink?" Tamara sobbed.

"Quick—get Anton!"

33

Eye for an Eye

Office of Max Parris

Alpha Technologies

1100 Hours

Without the two computers and business phone placed strategically on his large mahogany desk, Max's spacious office would be considered spartan—or a waste of one thousand square feet of prime office space.

Novak and Bing were communicating with Parris on their genius phones. "Yes, in forty-eight hours, our next threat will be a reality. I personally spoke with Hickler regarding the schedule. Be ready to capitalize on the widespread fatalities in your country. These incidents should prove beyond any doubt that your nations are under attack by unknown, ruthless enemies. It will become clear that only our defenses can stop the killings." Max secured his genius phone on his desk.

Next, Max reached for his intercom. "Please send Mr. Mischa Cantz into my office." Mischa should have some very agreeable news, based on a brief conversation the two had while Max was being chauffeured to the office.

"Come in, my good friend. I'm waiting to hear just how much your latest information is going to cost me." Parris laughed at his own joke.

"For once, I will let you set the price you'll pay for having that man Hull's wife in your special safekeeping sites—rumored to be under your control, which is beyond my understanding. That being said, my men have her under control, and with one call from me, she'll be delivered to you." Now Mischa was laughing at his own humor.

"You truly have her? What if I give you one million today and the balance when I need you to dispose of her? She's of limited value to me. Once I have the government contract, her husband will be powerless to damage me in any way." Mischa held out his hand to seal the agreement.

"We have a deal. You write me a check for one million dollars today, and a second one dated ninety days from now. I will contact my specially trained forces to deliver her to the address you specify." Mischa took his cell phone from his jacket pocket and dialed the number of his lead enforcer. He couldn't understand why the call went to voicemail—something strictly forbidden under Mischa's orders.

Turning to Max, he said, "Apparently there's something wrong with his phone. I'll try again in a few minutes. No need for me to bother you in your office. I'll wait outside." His words did little to reassure Max, who watched him leave with growing unease.

Once outside, Mischa tried dialing not once, but three times—without success.

***

Motel Laundry Room

1030 Hours

Tamara never saw the hand that slapped her face.

"You dirty bitch—you killed my brother." Anton raised his hand to deliver a second blow, this one powerful enough to break the ties binding her to the chair, sending her sprawling to the floor. Blood now flowed freely from her nose and mouth.

Anton never expected the bloodied woman's response.

"You fool. My husband is Roy Hull, and I know he's searching for me. The smartest thing you can do is untie me and set me free. If not, whatever happens to me, he will cut your heart out and shove it down your throat while it's still beating." Tamara knew this to be true, even if she wouldn't be alive to see it.

"Roy Hull? Never heard of him. If he's so courageous, how did he let you fall into our hands? I may not eat your heart, but I plan to do other, more pleasurable things with you before Mischa's people escort you to a less friendly site."

"That must be them now. How unfortunate—you'll never get to taste the bitter fruit you had planned for me. Just a minute, I'll open the door for you." Anton left the bleeding Tamara and walked to open the door.

"Anton, I have news for you…" Emily's voice was faint.

Anton opened the door—only to have Emily shoved into him, knocking them both to the ground. He opened his eyes to see a sword held perilously close to his left eye.

MadMan and Chasey followed Hull into the laundry room.

The two men assigned to guard Tamara rushed into the outer room with weapons drawn, ready for any emergency. They had heard the door open and the sound of bodies colliding. From where they stood, they could see Anton pinned to the ground by a deranged man screaming oaths at him with a sword inches from his eye.

In unison, the guards raised their weapons—just ten yards from their target.

They were one second too late. The two men collapsed on top of each other, shot dead.

Chasey and MadMan had burst in right behind Hull. True to their training, they had their Pit Vipers drawn and ready. No sound came from either weapon, but the two lifeless bodies proved that Hull had chosen the right men and the right tools for this mission.

"I'm only going to ask you one time—what have you done to my wife, Tamara?" Hull's voice roared with fury.

At that moment, he looked up to see Tamara shakily holding onto the doorframe to steady herself. It was immediately clear to Hull—from the blood streaming from her nose and lip—that she had been brutally beaten.

It was nothing but raw, animal instinct that caused Hull to thrust the blade through Anton's left eye, pinning his head to the floor.

Hull rose quickly and wrapped his arms around Tamara. He picked her up and gently placed her in a nearby chair. He returned briefly to Anton's body to retrieve and clean his sword.

"Dan, MadMan—I'll drive Tam's car back to base. She's in bad shape and needs immediate medical attention. You two take the chopper and ferry her back to Andrews. Stay with her until I return." His voice was as cold as the steel of his blade.

"No problem," MadMan replied. "I'll call Dr. Deer from the heli and arrange for her transportation. You take care of yourself."

MadMan laughed inwardly. It was the people who dared attack Hull that would need medical care.

Emily stood trembling, blood streaming down the left side of her face.

"I'm leaving you alive to tell your leader this—Roy Hull will never rest until he's in his grave." Hull held his blade close to Emily's left eye, making certain she would remember and report every word exactly.

Exiting the complex, Hull noticed two large SUVs entering just as he drove Tamara's Corvette back to Andrews.

34

Mischa's Reward

Andrews Air Force Base

April, 1300 Hours

I did the best I could with your wife's injuries. There will be no permanent damage. One or two more blows would have caused a concussion or worse. She has been sedated. Rest is the absolute best medicine I can prescribe, Donna Deer said, turning to Roy Hull—her longtime friend, best man at her wedding, and protector when necessary.

"She will never be alone while we are under attack. MadMan and Chasey will guard her around the clock. You are one of the few who knows what condition I was in when Ashley, my first wife, was hacked to death in Iraq. If Tamara had met a similar fate, my life would have been torn apart. What would have been the result? I shudder to even contemplate it." Roy was glued to his sleeping wife as he spoke.

John Ashley was stopped at the entrance of Andrews. The delay finally allowed him to contact Roy Hull with his cell phone.

"Thank God you answered. I've been calling you for the past two hours. My family may be in danger. I need to see you. I'm driving to your quarters as we speak," Ashley said, his voice strained and emotional.

***

Mischa Tover's Office

1300 Hours

"Emily, to say the very least, I am very disappointed in your failure." Mischa eyed her bloody ear with disgust in his voice. "You had four of my best men under your supervision to kidnap and bring me one lone female. Yet, when my men came to return her to my safekeeping, I found the four men assigned to you dead and blood streaming from where your left ear should be. Not a very appealing sight."

Mischa had no place in his organization for failure. Summoning one of the men who had escorted Emily into his office, he coldly instructed, "Make sure she suffers before you dispose of her in the incinerator at my ranch."

Emily let out a scream that could not be heard due to the soundproofing in Mischa's office.

"It was not my fault! That man—Hull—is the devil in human form. He stabbed Anton through his eye without thinking. It makes me feel better to tell you he is coming after you."

Mischa was extremely disappointed with Emily's behavior. He opened his desk drawer, took out his favorite Luger, and, aiming directly at Emily's forehead, fired twice.

"Find something to wrap her body in. I very much dislike blood on my office floor. Take her out of the building. My incinerator will be her final resting place as a reward for failure," Mischa ordered the four men who had picked up Emily from the motel.

***

Parris Office

1400 Hours

Maximillian "Max" Parris was, by nature and temperament, a person not given to rash judgments. Some minor events, individually, would not have been troubling. But more than once, he believed someone was monitoring his computer and phone.

When he had conceived this entire scheme to induce panic with a series of small fatal events, he had given serious thought to which organization or individual could have the extraordinary skill to uncover his plans. Only the famed Russian hacker, Georgi, was his technical equal.

Last month, he mentioned Georgi's name and location to Mischa. Mischa later reported the hacker had suffered a severe injury and was hospitalized with major bodily damage. Max was content with the outcome, although it had proven to be expensive.

The latest incidents didn't bother Max too much, but he believed his two comrades were not as technically savvy as he was. Reviewing the individuals assigned to Hull, he researched the names and credentials of Hull's team. One name stood out—Willi Pepovitch, from Moscow—who had attended advanced computer and software classes.

Max noted the man's name and placed a call to Mischa. It was probably a waste of money, but when contemplating billions in profits, he couldn't afford to be too cautious.

Andrews Air Force Base

Hull Team Complex

1400 Hours

A haggard and distraught John Ashley could scarcely hold the glass of water Hull had poured for him.

"Roy, earlier this morning, my father called me, telling me two men he had never seen were inspecting my home from the street. They were taking pictures—specifically of my two small daughters who were on their way to school. My father, fearing the worst, called me. He picked them up from school and feels confident they are safe for the moment. My mother and wife remain at my parents' home.

"I informed the President. His first question was, 'What the hell are you doing here and not on your way to your parents' home to protect your family?' I asked my personal Secret Service bodyguard to contact their counterparts in the New York area to provide protection until I arrive.

"Roy, we are dealing with an unknown, well-connected, well-financed, and extremely dangerous enemy. When you told me what happened to your wife, I became convinced—they will stop at nothing to reach their goals, whatever they are. I'm flying out of here in half an hour. If you need the President, use his number." He took a small notepad from his jacket pocket. "You have my cell number, and I have your secret number. If I need your help, I'll call."

Ashley shook Hull's hand, picked up his travel bag, and walked out to the staff car waiting for him.

***

Pepovitch Computer Module

1400 Hours

Willi Pepovitch was exhausted. After speaking with Hull, he had been working nonstop, using the information he had gathered to trace people or business enterprises that might profit from the isolated, deadly events occurring worldwide.

Fueled by coffee and hours of persistence, he had finally found links between five or six key entities. Excited, he printed his findings and placed them in a folder. He knew this information had to get into Hull's hands.

Hurrying out of the computer room with the folder clutched tightly in his right hand, Willi nearly ran over a man in the hallway—a man he didn't recognize.

"Sorry, I was in a hurry and didn't see you," Willi apologized, still gripping the folder.

Then it struck him—no one but members of Hull's immediate group were allowed in the facility. His pulse quickened. Spinning toward the exit, he saw the same man now running after him.

Not good, Willi thought grimly.

Across the way, he spotted MadMan in the stairwell of the adjoining building.

"MadMan!" Willi screamed, sprinting toward him. The unknown man was gaining on him with every step.

Willi's heart pounded. He remembered what had happened to Blake and the other FBI agent. He pushed harder, trying to escape. He could hear and feel how close the man was now.

Out of the corner of his eye, he caught the glint of a steel-bladed knife—**inches** from his neck.

I do not want to die anywhere but Mother Russia.

Suddenly, a flash of brown slammed into him. Willi hit the ground hard, certain his life was over. He braced for the steel to pierce his spine.

But instead, he heard a voice: "Sorry I had to knock you down, but your attacker's blade was only inches from your spine. He's in no position to hurt anyone now. I cut his throat with his own knife."

Dan Chasey reached down and offered his hand to the stunned but very much alive Willi, helping him to his feet.

It took Willi five minutes or more to catch his breath.

His first reaction: **I'm happy to be alive.**

His second: **What did I get myself into? I should be drinking vodka in my apartment.**

His third: **What kind of ninja training lets someone throw me to the ground while simultaneously killing my attacker?**

Finally, he managed to blurt out, "I need to see Hull immediately."

35

Past and Present

Kim Hickler's Compound

Bahía Blanca, Argentina

May 1

Cold beads of perspiration trickled down both men's necks. Although the outside temperature was extremely warm and humid, Braun and Kessler had been summoned by Hickler without warning. Walking to the Hickler compound, located on the western edge of Bahía Blanca, both men knew—nothing good ever happened to subordinates called to appear before Hickler.

"What delayed your arrival? I notified you fifteen minutes ago that I wanted to meet with you." Kim Hickler's eyes pierced directly into the two men's innermost thoughts. "I require your input on our next operation."

Braun volunteered to answer first. "My teams in each country need only the target area selected. The drone operators must be within fifty kilometers of the site. We were instructed by Kessler not to have outside people investigate or examine the dead bodies for two hours. My enforcement detail wears Hazmat suits to protect themselves from the deceased, who can cause severe injury or death."

"Excellent! We cannot afford any type of investigation after our final test. Billions of dollars are at stake for our cause." Hickler raised her voice for emphasis. "Kessler, what limits your production of our deadly scent?"

Kessler was surprised by her question. He had reported directly to her about the numerous intricate distillation processes involved in creating the deadly gas in semi-liquid form. In past discussions, Hickler had never shown an interest in how the gas was formed.

"Fräulein Hickler, we have a very small laboratory. There is limited room for the necessary equipment. Training skilled scientists to work with these deadly compounds takes years. I hope you understand?"

Kessler feared Hickler would draw her Luger and shoot him in the forehead at close range.

"Enough of your excuses!" Hickler screamed at both men. "Braun, by tomorrow at noon, I need your plans for increasing drone production by a thousand times your current rate. Kessler, during the same time, I will require a detailed plan for increasing your output by the same amount. Let me worry about space and personnel decisions. I want to explain the next stage in our mission only once."

"What you are proposing is sheer lunacy," Kessler protested.

"Kessler is correct, Fräulein Hickler. Our facilities will not allow additional units to be produced in Bahía Blanca," Braun added, trying to reinforce Kessler's ill-worded response.

Both men realized other staff members had been put to death for disagreeing with her.

"In a few minutes, I will introduce you to one of the world's most powerful men. Very few people know his real name. To the best of my knowledge, only myself and one other understand his true purpose in life. He will explain what is expected of you. After he meets with us, you must carry out his orders fully and without question."

Hickler turned sharply and left the room.

"Braun, I am worried. Very worried. I always believed Hickler was in charge. We have no choice but to obey," Kessler said, echoing Braun's thoughts completely.

***

Andrews Air Force Base

Task Force Operations Room

May 1, 1100 Hours

Roy Hull was concentrating on a chart Ashley had left for him. *Interesting,* he thought. He added his analysis to the computer model he had constructed.

Hearing the door open, he was amazed, surprised, and slightly amused by the sight of Willi's face.

"Willi, either you met an angry husband or a grizzly bear, judging by the patchwork of cuts and bruises on your face."

"This is a crazy country. The protection at your military base leaves much to be desired. If my good new friend Chasey had not been so vigilant, the information I have so painfully gathered for you would never have been made available.

"Doctor Deer, who has great insights into threat options, and I have worked to the point of exhaustion attempting to use the information you provided after your California trip."

Willi selected three sheets of paper from his folder, each highlighted with a different color fastener.

"Can you explain exactly what these different sheets and colors represent in simple terms? I have my own analysis based on conversations I had with various members of the Red Cell." Hull was puzzled by the strange notations Willi had scrawled on each.

"As I said before, Dr. Deer provided the first clue. She asked if I could determine the time intervals between attacks in three different countries. My timing is strictly based on reports gathered from data secured on national government computers. Before you ask, I've taken the necessary safeguards to protect myself from being traced.

"The first sheet illustrates the different colors of countries and the time lapse between attacks. Russia is always the first country to be attacked, approximately four hours after China, which is approximately four hours after this country."

Willi pointed to the different colors representing time and countries.

"Willi, are you telling me that if we receive notice Russia has been attacked, we have eight hours to assemble, pack necessary equipment, and be ready to leave before the next attack strikes our country?" Hull was shaking his head in disbelief.

"With only one highly important factor to be considered," Willi laughed. "Where?"

Willi turned over the second multicolored sheet. Hull could see this one was very different from the first. Names in blue, countries in red, immediately stood out.

Hull raised a question to Willi. "What does this tell me?"

"It answers the question you raised on your return from the meeting with the Red Cell group—who benefits from the brutal murders?

"Using Jaz and John as a resource, we determined the one group or person in each country who would benefit the most. We started with all the large defense contractors in each country. As I mentioned, the three of us—using our military contacts—easily narrowed the list to one person in each country who stands to benefit most from these attacks. They are circled in black for your ease of review."

Willi continued speaking. "There is one element that has me baffled. The three men I highlighted communicate often by phone. It's quite simple to follow their communications. The third sheet lists each call, usually from the source in this country.

"What troubles me is that I cannot listen to their conversations. Someone has designed a communication system with an extremely powerful encryption safeguard—one so advanced that even someone with my skills cannot break through it."

36

History Lesson

Fuerth Compound

Kim Hickler's private office

1100 Hours

Ernst and Braun glanced at each other, reluctant to speak. Hickler had created a sense of foreboding in both men. The door opened, and a thin, older man entered. His bearing was old-style military—erect, hawk-like eyes, and wearing a monocle.

"My name is Richard Hickler. Yes, Hickler is my daughter. Refer to me as General X for discussion purposes. Your work and past efforts were part of a strategy put together by true *Wolfhead* patriots—not afraid to think boldly about the future. As the last worldwide war was ending, the high command was shaping plans for complete world domination. You two patriots are the most important and essential individuals to complete our nation's destiny."

General X's deep bass voice never changed its impassioned tone as he addressed Ernst and Braun.

"Herr General, we have demonstrated our capabilities to the Russians, Chinese, and American businesspeople who are financing our efforts. They are now prepared to spend even more for our next, larger demonstration. What more are you expecting?" Ernst asked, not necessarily expecting an answer.

"Precisely the reason I was ordered to speak with you," the General said. "The master plan was to gain a level of expertise with others bearing the cost of the very expensive development. My understanding is that you are being paid to unleash your weapons at sites designated by the people employing you. They, in turn, are the beneficiaries of extremely large government contracts to prevent future attacks on their countries and citizens.

"Of course, after they secure their monies, they will have no further need for your services. But I ask you—what if we merely threaten to plan a future attack? That would improve our bargaining position. They will be forced to offer us additional sums of money, or we will be able to strike any target at any time.

"Some would call it extortion, but the beautiful element is that the people paying the blackmail cannot go to the authorities without giving away their own treachery. Now, is that not correct, gentlemen?"

The General carefully removed his monocle as he posed the question to the two men.

"General," Braun shakily volunteered, "Hickler does not involve us in any planning. She dictates our delivery schedule and places my sentries and pilots where she needs them. We have little knowledge of any financial dealings."

"Very well. Now prepare yourselves to become full members of our plan to retake the world for our new leaders. The *Wolfhead*'s master plan was conceived to have the most powerful countries wage war against each other, weakening their defenses until we are strong enough to overpower them with your creations.

"After I leave, I will visit another country—one dedicated to overthrowing the world's oppressors with unlimited scientific and manufacturing resources. Once I have their cooperation, I will return for the two of you to lead the new operations. I have ordered Hickler to provide you with additional security."

General X turned abruptly, leaving the meeting with a smile on his face.

"Ernst, what do you make of our strange General's news—being vital members of a plan to retake the world for our cause?"

"It worries me more than I can tell you. Not obeying would bring instant death to our families and ourselves," Ernst replied honestly, fully aware of the threat.

37

Identification

Andrews Air Force Base

Team Planning Center

May 3

Hull, Chasey, and Madman gathered around Willi's computer. "This is why I asked you to meet with me," Willi began, pointing to a series of names and numbers on his computer screen.

"My research developed algorithms that revealed some remarkably interesting and unusual patterns. Using the logic Hull brought back from California, I altered my computer search parameters to focus on individuals or organizations that stand to benefit most from providing protection against unknown threats.

"I used John and Jaz to help me identify those individuals in their country. We were amazed when the answers became so apparent. After they left, I used the names to cross-check activity between the three. The American individual is extremely clever. I couldn't find a pattern in his calls. He uses several highly advanced signal-transferring techniques when placing his calls. As I told you before, his communications are safeguarded against intrusion.

"However, the other two individuals are not as careful in placing their phone calls. It became readily apparent that the three were in constant communication with each other. Many of the phone calls were initiated by the American contact. It was almost impossible for me to trace the physical travels of the foreign agents, but the American's movements were much more productive.

"He makes frequent visits to a nearby office building with this address and weekly trips outside of Washington to a farm he owns. Uncharacteristically, he used his private plane to fly to Bahia Blanca, Argentina, last week. His pilot had to file a flight plan with the FAA."

Willi finished with a dramatic gesture, standing up and taking a bow before the three men.

Madman was the first to acknowledge the importance of Willi's research.

"Willi, you just provided us with a starting point in our search to stop the unknown deadly threats before they appear again. Are there any other odd bits of information you found in your search?"

"Not in locating the three main subjects," Willi replied, clearly reluctant to share more details—especially those gathered through illegal tampering in government files. "I've been working with Doctor Deer, reading the law enforcement and medical reports from this country, plus what I could electronically pilfer from the Chinese and Russians. She's one smart lady.

"She noticed references in all three countries of personnel in protective equipment—Hazmat suits—being on-site where the dead bodies were found, even before law enforcement officials arrived. She posed the question to me: Was the time sequence in my illegal searches accurate?

"We decided—or rather, the good doctor decided—to discuss it later with Roy. She had to return to the hospital. Several of her patients required her very extensive skills. She'll contact Roy later when time permits."

Willi handed his documents to Hull. "Could I ask one of you gentlemen to escort me back to my work area? One deadly attempt on my life is enough for today," he added, remembering his hasty exit earlier that morning.

"Let me escort Willi," Chasey offered. "I need to work on my Pit Viper. With the number of accessories offered, I need more time to become familiar with all of them. The silencer fits and acts much differently than any I've used in the past. Come on, Willi."

Hull waited until the two had left before reaching for his cell phone.

"Madman, Donna needs to speak with me privately. When we were younger, if one of us wanted to speak in private, we'd use the excuse that someone needed our help. Donna must have noticed something she didn't want to share with Willi."

Hull dialed her number, waiting for his friend to answer.

"Madman, can you track who was sent to kill Willi? I must wait for Donna to contact me."

"Absolutely, no problem," Madman replied. "We must have been compromised before we even arrived at Andrews. Can I speak with Ashley? I know he made an unexpectedly rapid exit from Washington. I didn't want to bother you with the reason, but speaking to him would assist my efforts to locate and end our threat."

"Here is his private number," Hull said, handing him a card with Ashley's number printed on it.

Gathering his thoughts, Hull reviewed more closely the coded sheets Willi had left behind. Willi had pinpointed times and dates of calls between the three men. A sudden realization flashed in Hull's mind. Reaching for Ashley's report on the previous months' attacks, it became obvious—the number of calls spiked the day before each deadly attack occurred.

His second private cell phone alerted him to a call.

"Hull here. Who is this? I don't recognize the number."

"Roy, this is Donna. I used a friend's phone to contact you. Willi's data raised some remarkably interesting and alarming questions I need to discuss with you privately. My Native American instincts are warning me—someone is watching me. The hospital doesn't allow weapons. My revolver is locked in my car."

"Donna, can you move to a secure area? I can drive down to you in thirty minutes." Hull's mind was racing for a solution. "What condition is Agent Blake in? I know Agent Peters has secretly hidden his service revolver in his room. The FBI should have guards posted outside."

"I can request a security guard to escort me to Blake's private room. He's in much better shape. Meet me in his room when you reach the hospital. I'll tell him he's on guard duty—it'll speed up his healing," Donna laughed.

"Peters, are you fit for action?" Hull asked, grabbing his sports jacket as he spoke. "Meet me in the parking lot. Bring your weapon."

Doctor Donna Running Deer contacted security as Hull had instructed. She waited patiently in her office on the top floor of the hospital. Fifteen minutes had passed since she placed the call. Stepping into the corridor outside her office, she became alarmed at the lack of activity. The eerie stillness raised her fears.

Dialing security, she received a constant busy signal.

Who could she contact without raising suspicion?

Drawing from years of knowing Hull, she texted him, **"I skin them, you kill them,"** well aware that anyone monitoring her communications would view it as a friendly joke.

Donna had no doubt in her mind—she was being forcibly isolated in her office.

She thought back to the personnel she had interacted with at the hospital. Other than her close medical associates, she had only spoken to a security guard when entering the building.

Willi's files were hidden from view, marked only with Hull's name and hers on the front page. She found it odd when the security guard had asked to search her purse and file folder.

Hull was alerted to Donna's text. He knew immediately she was in trouble. From their childhood, "You kill them, I skin them—no fat" was their secret phrase to signal danger. The order was reversed this time, a clear message.

Hull texted her back: *"Build a fort, stay low, get your running shoes on."*

Dialing the private, secret number, he calmly stated, "I need a police escort from Andrews to Johns Hopkins in five minutes." He adjusted his new Pit Viper holster to his back and rushed out to Donna's Jag.

A police officer held up his hand, stopping Hull from leaving.

"I just received a message from my boss that the President wants Roy Hull to have a private escort to Johns Hopkins. Are you Roy Hull?"

Hull showed him the President's card with his name on it.

"Stay in your car. Get ready to rock and roll."

Hull smiled. "Turn off your sirens and flashing lights two blocks before pulling into the hospital. Head for the ER section. After I park, you can leave. I'll buy you a beer when I have time to explain."

The police officer laughed out loud. "Captain Dan Mulvaney, the President's Director of Security. And it'll be a full dinner for two at a restaurant of my choice. I was hoping to celebrate my wedding anniversary when the President personally called me and asked me to divide your escort."

***

Reading Hull's message, Donna understood his coded text: *Barricade yourself as long as possible. When danger is too close, look for a way to escape and get to cover where you can run if necessary. I'll find you by listening for an eagle call.*

Her first task was to change into jeans, a sweatshirt, and running shoes, which she kept in her office. Hurriedly dressing, she then secured her office as best she could. First, she pushed her heavy oak desk in front of the door. Then she added more weight by moving her file cabinet behind the desk.

Not having a weapon was a major handicap. Picking through her hospital supplies, she isolated a scalpel and a large syringe, carefully filling it with a powerful muscle relaxant and sedative—midazolam.

Suddenly, extremely violent male voices began shouting outside her office door.

"The door is locked. We'll have to kick it in!"

A loud thud of someone kicking the door was immediately followed by a shrill cry of pain, masked with an obscene oath.

"Stand back," another louder male voice barked. "Mischa ordered me to make sure this doctor doesn't leave the hospital alive."

Donna understood the next sound—*ch-chk*—was a shotgun shell being pumped into the chamber, ready to fire. She dropped to the floor just as the first blast tore a huge hole through her door. One more, and they'd decimate the barrier, leaving her defenseless.

Flattening herself to the floor, Donna crawled to the rear entrance of her office, which led to the parking area. Before opening the door, she crouched into a fighting position. Behind her, men burst into her office, shouting crude threats about what they planned to do to her before killing her.

As she slowly turned the doorknob, it suddenly flew open. A man, stationed to guard against her escape, stood there. He was scanning the room, unaware that Donna was crouched just below his line of sight.

Without hesitation, she leapt from her position and drove the syringe deep into his jugular. The man tried to grab her as he stumbled backward, attempting to delay her until the others caught up. But Donna had planned well—midazolam injected directly into the jugular worked fast. Within seconds, the man was glassy-eyed and half-paralyzed.

She shoved him down the stairs and sprinted into the darkness. Her heart pounded so fiercely that she couldn't be sure, but she thought gunfire rang out behind her as she fled.

Donna recalled her father's words: *"When threatened, seek high ground with cover from the forest."* Hull's father had taught her and Roy the same principle during their childhood hunting trips. *"High ground is always your friend."*

Now, through perspiration-filled eyes, Donna ran for any cover she could find near the parking lot—and beyond.

38

Scheduling Death

Fuerth compound

Kim Hickler complex

Bahia Blanca, Argentina

Hickler had specifically designed the Fuerth compound to repel outsiders from prying eyes and to prevent careless wandering by townspeople. Storefronts and office buildings shielded any direct line of sight. Carefully placed slots for automatic weapons were concealed behind decorative multi-colored bricks.

Ernst and Braun were once again together—this time in fear—waiting for Hickler to make an appearance. The elderly male visitor was clearly under Hickler's dominance.

The door opened, and two large men with close-cropped hair entered, followed by Hickler.

The two men flanked Hickler as she began to speak.

"These men, and others, are your new protection. My friend and I discussed security arrangements for each of you," Hickler said, pausing. "Because you two hold and control all of the science and technology required to finally impose our fundamental beliefs on the world. We failed once. We cannot afford to fail a second time."

"Why do we need personal protection?" Ernst asked. "Fuerth is heavily guarded. We've subtly disguised our real purpose by adding a variety of entertainment locations and fine restaurants to blind others from our manufacture of new and improved methods of delivering death to millions. Several generations have labored most of their lives for us to reach our current high state of readiness."

"Exactly. I called this meeting to give you our new schedule. You have three days to equip and man these locations." She held out a lined sheet of paper with the names of the locations, along with the number of people attending each of the three venues.

"The aim of these demonstrations," Hickler continued, "is to rapidly convince the governments of each location to fund the organizations providing us with the resources you demanded to complete your experiments."

She added emphasis as she circled the areas to be targeted, underlining in red the anticipated number of deaths.

Braun's eyes opened and closed slowly, staggered by the numbers Hickler had written. Ernst stuttered, visibly shaken by the forecasted death toll.

"I don't believe we have the necessary material and equipment," he said.

"No excuses!" Hickler snapped. "I've given you one additional day to produce extra quantities of our unique lethal solution. Once we establish our superiority and stealth, we will no longer need our three benefactors—those who've reaped large benefits from our efforts."

She took her pen and circled the date and number again for emphasis.

39

Donna in Danger

One block from Johns Hopkins Hospital

2000 Hours

Turn off your siren and lights. Drive to the emergency room exit. Whoever is threatening our friend doesn't need to know we arrived.

Mulvaney complied with Hull's command, stopping at the entrance to the emergency room as directed.

Peters, rifle slung over her left shoulder, jumped out of the car before it came to a full stop. "I'm going to check on Agent Blake. If those people are hunting Donna, Blake may be in serious trouble." She moved like a jungle cat, weaving in and out of various doors leading to Blake's room on the first floor.

Hull waited for the car to come to a complete stop. Stepping from the vehicle, he handed Mulvaney a plastic card.

"I'll tell the President what a great job you did on your special night. The credit card I just gave you is my personal one. It's a bit unusual—it has no spending limit. No need to return it to me. Treat your wife to a great time. Just hand it over to the President when you're finished with it."

Hull checked his Pit Viper while walking to the entrance.

It didn't take long for Hull to realize something was tragically wrong. The emergency area was completely deserted. Surveying the surroundings, he soon spotted a pool of blood at the front side of the reception desk.

Proceeding slowly, he saw a body hidden from the entrance windows. There was no doubt—the security officer on duty had been shot several times. A heightened sense of urgency came over him. Donna was in serious danger.

Standing up, he heard a banging noise coming from one of the rooms in the back. Still cautious, unsure of who or where the assailants were, Hull crawled toward the door. Voices were shouting and screaming for help.

Standing erect, he tried the door. Meeting resistance, he acted on reflex, delivering a series of kicks and battering the door open. Inside, medical personnel and patients were milling around, thanking Hull for rescuing them.

A person wearing hospital clothing with a name tag reading *Dr. Alexis* stepped in front of Hull.

"They asked me which floor Dr. Deer's office was on. One of them held a gun to my forehead when I shouted, 'Fifth floor.' At that point, the men herded us into this room at gunpoint. Sully, our security officer, was shot at point-blank range when he ran to help us."

Leaping two steps at a time, Hull's concern deepened as he saw no one in the corridors of the floors he passed. Checking his weapon, he hurriedly attached the suppressor.

Peering carefully around the entrance to the fifth floor, he spotted a lone sentry holding an automatic weapon, guarding what remained of Deer's shattered door. Placing his weapon behind his back, Hull stepped into the guard's view.

Hull shouted, "What in the hell happened here?"

The guard motioned for Hull to stop. "Nobody's allowed on this floor unless you have permission. My boss mentioned nothing about a visitor, so I won't ask twice for you to leave. We wanted a meeting with the good doctor, but she wasn't seeing patients tonight. My friends, as you can see, went to change her mind."

His attempt at humor ended abruptly when Hull's Pit Viper came out from hiding and slammed a .357 round into his heart—almost without a sound.

With the office door already shattered, Hull keyed in his halo communication mouthpiece.

"Peters, what's Blake's condition? I need you and Blake to guard the emergency room and its personnel. I'm going after the men pursuing Donna."

Peters responded, "Blake wants you to know he's mobile and mean. He killed two men who were assigned to silence him. I may have forgotten to tell you—I returned his service revolver to him while he was hospitalized. We're on our way over."

Hull jumped over the desk that Deer had used to block the entrance to her office. Glancing at the scattered books and equipment, he understood Donna had used everything at her disposal to slow her attackers.

The rear door had been flung open. As Hull passed through, he stumbled over the body of a man with an oversized hypodermic needle protruding from his neck.

Typical Donna, he thought as he ran toward the open door leading to the parking area.

The parking lot was only dimly lit. The moon was rising over a grove of trees and shrubbery on the west end of the lot. Hull scanned all possible hiding places. He knew Donna would remember her father's warning: *"When in doubt, use high ground and forest to protect yourself."*

The sound of gunfire and muzzle flashes from the tree line confirmed his worst fears. His mind was racing as he frantically tried to save his childhood friend.

Strategically, he had two advantages: Donna's pursuers didn't know he was tracking them, and he understood her tactics.

Proceeding into the forest, he pushed through dense shrubs and weeds. He had to signal Donna without calling her name. He pursed his lips and sent out the sound of a wounded rabbit. As children, they had spent hours perfecting that sound to lure wolves and foxes for their pelts. He repeated it.

Close to his position, gunshots rang out.

"She's over to my right," a man's voice broke the silence. "My flashlight caught a glimpse of her. She's staying close to the ground. Circle to my right, and we'll have her trapped. How much did Mischa promise us if we delivered her dead body tonight?"

Donna instantly recognized Hull's unique signal. She had few hiding places left, and the men following her were no amateurs. They were methodical, carefully limiting any escape routes.

From her vantage point, she could see them. They moved in a pattern, sweeping side to side to cover every area.

Lying flat on her back for concealment, she responded with the same wounded-rabbit call Hull had used. The sound had just left her lips when a flashlight blinded her, and a second pair of arms jolted her upright from her prone position.

"We've got her!" shouted the man with the flashlight. Donna was blinded by the beam directed into her eyes.

"Move!" he barked, forcing her toward a clearing near the parking area. He gave her a shove, sending her sprawling. Donna stumbled and fell in the dense underbrush. Both men laughed as she struggled to get up.

"Make that sound again," sneered one of the men. "Maybe some miracle will stop us from slitting your throat when we reach our friends."

The second man started to laugh—until he suddenly felt a sharp pain in his lower right abdomen. As his companion and Donna watched, blood began to stream from his mouth. He collapsed to the ground.

"The miracle man has arrived." Hull held his blood-soaked sword in the second man's face. "Mischa will not be happy when you report I took one of his best men. Call your friends. I want to meet them." Hull left no room for doubt—he wanted instant action.

Donna Running Deer was famous for her quiet and studious demeanor. It was quite unexpected when she made a fist and smashed it into the man's nose. Blood gushed and pooled on the man's shirt.

"I taught her that when we were growing up. She was a quick study," Hull laughed.

Hull motioned for Donna to walk slowly. Whispering, he said, "We haven't heard from his friends. Keep our friend company. If he decides to make a sound—which I doubt—hit him harder."

Moving deliberately, a trait instilled by his Indian brothers, Hull kept alert. A human form suddenly appeared. Hull quickly removed his prized sword from its resting place along his spine. A second form joined the first, causing him to shift his position.

"Gentlemen, you can put your hands on your head," Hull said, rising from his concealed position.

The two armed men were caught by surprise and offered no resistance. Neither said a word; they simply stood studying Hull's face in the dim light. The sixth sense that had saved Hull many times began to resonate. The two captured men stood grinning at each other, both expecting to be free within minutes.

A single shot rang out.

Hull turned to see a man with a rifle crumple slowly to the ground.

"You can thank me later, Hull." FBI Agent Peters stepped from the shadows. "The guy hiding behind you was ready to level you with his weapon."

She made it sound like a joke as she moved toward Hull and Donna.

"Blake is standing guard over the emergency room personnel. By now, the police must have arrived. We should escort your friend with the bloody nose to get it treated—though he might not receive the tender loving care this hospital is known for," Peters quipped, making Hull and Donna smile.

"Before we turn him over to the police, I want to ask him some questions—like how Mischa always knows where we are," Hull said, stepping inches from the man's face, his sword held at eye level. The other two men were transfixed with fear as Agent Peters waved her rifle at them.

"All I'll tell you is my name is Levi. That, and the fact that Mischa's attorneys will have me out on bond within hours. Just like these other two. He controls law enforcement, lawyers, and other government officials. I choose not to answer your questions," Levi sneered. "You and the FBI agent are law enforcement with your codes of conduct. You can't let me give you any information. My nose is still dripping blood. Hurry and take me to the police and the medical staff gathered in front of the hospital." He ended by spitting blood at Hull and laughing.

"Unfortunately, what he says is technically correct," Peters said to Hull. "Any damage we inflict gives him an easy appeal—and probably freedom."

Hull nodded. "Yes, being in law enforcement shackles our efforts to figure out how Mischa always stays one step ahead. Today, Chasey had to rescue Willi from someone who found out we're stationed at Andrews. I don't like it any more than you do."

Donna turned to Hull. "Do you still have that small Walther .38 in your ankle holster—the one I made for you when you entered SEAL training?"

"Yes. I never leave home without it. Why do you ask?" he replied, wondering why she'd ask something she already knew.

"Would you hand it to me? I've had my office destroyed, had to kill a man to escape, and ran for my life until you rescued me—just in case you're wondering."

"No problem." Hull bent down to free the weapon from its hiding place and handed it to Donna as he stood.

"I've listened to what Peters and you were discussing with Levi. From what I understand, you two have legal constraints on how to properly ask him how his boss and organization acquire intelligence. I don't have those same restrictions."

Pointing the gun at Levi's knee, she said, "Since I'm a civilian and was under threat of being killed, I can act accordingly. Levi, I'm only going to ask you once—politely—to answer what my two friends asked."

Levi gave Donna a bloody grin. "Nothing you can do will make me betray my friends."

"I was hoping you'd say that," Donna said slowly. "I grew up learning to shoot before I even started school. I'm a Native American—my people have been persecuted for centuries. And I'm a doctor. I know every pain point in your body. Most people think shooting a knee is the worst pain, but I can tell you—it's your ankle. Do you want to continue your silence? Because I assure you, I can damage your ankle so badly that only amputation will save your life. My alibi? You tried to kill me, and I was protecting myself."

Levi's eyes widened. "You wouldn't dare shoot me. You're a woman. And a doctor. I have no fear."

Before he could finish, Donna fired two shots into Levi's right ankle, shattering it into bits of bone and flesh. She followed by placing her leg firmly on the wounded area.

Hull turned to Peters. "I believe Donna may have persuaded Levi to cooperate."

Rolling on the ground in agony, Levi's screams pierced the air. "What do you want to know? Just keep that bitch away from me!"

Levi's two accomplices stood in shock, their mouths and eyes wide, unable to believe what had just happened. When Donna planted her foot on the injured ankle, one of them vomited.

Hull stood Levi upright. "If you don't answer my questions, Peters and I will walk away and let my 'mad friend' punish you beyond belief. Do you understand?"

Levi nodded frantically, ready to comply.

Peters had been right. Law enforcement officials from various agencies had taken over protective services for the hospital. She motioned for a few medical staff to join the group and explained that the man writhing on the ground was one of the attackers and needed medical attention before being handcuffed. The other two went willingly with the police, thinking escape from the deranged doctor could not come soon enough.

FBI Agent Harrison Blake joined them, a small bandage over his left eye. "Roy, I'm not going back to my room. Either I leave with you, or I return to my apartment."

"You're coming with us. Our enemy is far larger than I initially thought. If you haven't lost your edge, I need you back at Andrews."

Turning to Donna, he asked, "Can you commandeer an ambulance for their return to Andrews? If so, I'll drive your car back."

"My car keys are in my purse—in my office. Stay with me, and I'll give them to you."

Hull's phone blinked. He answered, then his expression darkened.

"What? Willi has disappeared? How could that happen? We're on our way back." He ended the call and turned to the others. "It's urgent we return immediately. Donna, ride with me. Willi is missing. He gave me the information I need to share with you."

40

How it Happens

US Highway 295 S

John Hopkins hospital to Andrews Air Force base

2200 Hours

Levi shared information I never considered possible. He said the upper echelons of the government are saturated with personnel who have little or no loyalty to this country, Hull spoke slowly, attempting to gauge the potential damage they could cause. "I purposely wanted to discuss the information Willi shared with me before your attackers threatened you."

"Willi, using both legal and illegal technical protocols, found a pattern in the unknown attacks causing limited but increasing deaths in China, Russia, and our country. There is a definite time lag between each country being attacked, based on his searches. We may not be able to stop the attack on China, but we might be in a position to defend against attacks in Russia and the United States."

Donna responded, "Willi and I believe the attacks leave no trace of the chemicals used to murder individuals, or how they are delivered. But we formed an educated guess from interviews with first responders. Personnel dressed in hazmat suits are positioned to prevent close inspection of the dead—both human and animal. Willi found the medical examiner's report from each incident, pointing out an eight-hour time difference between the countries. I need to be at the site of the next attack in this country to discover exactly what is occurring."

"Donna, once we return to Andrews, I'm assigning two bodyguards to you. Do not move without them. It's obvious your talents and expertise are known to Mischa, which makes you a threat to his plans. Do you have enough hazmat suits for your guards and protectors?"

"Once we arrive at Andrews, I'll call my head nurse and have her give the equipment and clothes to our delivery service. That shouldn't be a problem. Can you arrange for John Tsia to be one of my bodyguards? He gave us quite a show the other night with his 'shooting stars,' which would give me a sense of security. Tamara was just as impressed as I was by his talents," Donna laughed aloud at Hull's pained expression.

The ambulance Donna had requested was parked near the entrance to the group's living quarters. Donna and Hull smiled when they noticed Agent Blake gesturing to MadMan and another man they didn't recognize. Blake used his hands to describe in detail how he had shot the two men in the hospital.

The second man had a long black beard, unkempt hair, dirty jeans, and a sweatshirt reading *University of Miami 1984*. Hull was disturbed by the unknown man's presence. He had given strict instructions that no unidentified man or woman was to be allowed anywhere near their living quarters.

"Blake was describing Donna's non-textbook questioning approach," MadMan said as he held out his hand to Hull. "The good news is we found Willi—or rather, Willi found us. He was watching aircraft land and take off from the control tower."

"How could Willi gain access to the control tower?" Hull asked sharply. "It's one of the most secure buildings in this complex."

"I authorized his entrance," John Ashley remarked. "Don't let these clothes fool you; my word still carries weight on government grounds." Ashley extended his hand to shake a now-bewildered Roy Hull. "These are my hunting clothes. The men threatening my family went underground when my friends started protecting them. Rather than join them at my parents' home, I rented a cheap motel room at the edge of town. My appearance and living conditions kept me off the radar."

He continued, "The two men finally emerged yesterday, following my father and daughters to school. I never asked them why or what their mission was. I followed them to their motel. Behind closed doors, I started to question why they were following my daughters. The men went tight-lipped and stoic. I was running out of time and patience until I remembered a tactic that worked well in Iraq."

"I screwed the suppressor onto my Pit Viper and placed it at the throat of one of them. I asked the question one more time to the man who could speak. When he refused to answer, I blew his friend's head completely off—blood everywhere. Then I placed the weapon in the second man's mouth. His eyes went wide. He couldn't talk fast enough after that."

"He mentioned a man named Mischa, who commands a large number of ex-military and intelligence agents. Mischa takes orders and payment from numerous criminal partners. I reported to the President, who told me to take a few days off. I figured—who better to spend time with than your group to get up to speed on current developments?"

"Your wardrobe certainly fooled me. Just who are you?" Hull had worked with enough military units to know that Ashley's training far surpassed standard ranger expertise. "Your beard, long hair, and contact lenses give you a completely different profile. We can use your knowledge and authority to plan our next moves. It's great to see you again," Hull said with a smile.

"It's better if you don't know anything more about me," Ashley said quietly. "Plausible deniability," he added with a grin.

***

Bahía Blanca Airport

2300 Hours

Kim Hickler was busy—almost paranoid—making last-minute arrangements to load the three Boeing 747s designated to transport the chemicals and drones to the selected areas in the three targeted countries.

"Braun, are your lead personnel fully briefed on how to load and operate the larger ships we're using? Do you feel it's necessary to accompany them?"

"The operation of the new drones is similar to the ones we've used in previous missions. The most critical difference is loading much larger amounts of Kessler's gas. We've rehearsed the loading sequence many times. I have no fear of failure. The special guards in protective suits will be stationed to prevent outsiders from inspecting what kills the people and animals at your selected sites," Braun said emphatically.

"Just remember," Hickler replied, "if things fail, I'll have to find another aircraft specialist."

41

Willi's Analysis

Special Operations Room

Andrews Air Force Base

1400 hours

Willi Pepovitch stood before his computer screen. At his request, only Hull, MadMan, Chasey, Ashley, and Donna were allowed to join him.

"As I mentioned in an earlier meeting, I was successful in hacking into the Chinese and Russian individuals we suspect are partners in this scheme. The American, Max Parris, has installed security protocols more severe than any I have ever encountered. Using a fake website featuring prestigious yachts—the type favored by the Chinese official—I embedded a virus which allows me to access his communications with other parties.

"When he contacted the Russian, the virus was unknowingly downloaded to the Russian's computer. Again, I was stymied from learning additional critical information. They always use the security phone for those elements of the plan. Those phones are safely protected against any and all attempts I have made to breach them."

Pointing to objects on the screen, he scanned his notes. "Earlier this evening, I requested Ashley redirect a satellite to monitor airline activity from Bahia Blanca Airport. These images confirmed my earlier findings: this town is the hub of whatever actions are taking place in China, Russia, and the United States. The technicians in the center were tracing each flight and were to provide the landing destination of each plane.

"From the research, Donna and I were able to piece together some locations in China that will feel the first effects of the attack. As I mentioned before, we cannot pinpoint exactly where the attack will occur, but by studying the pattern of previous attacks, we can make a meaningful estimate of where the attacks will occur after China suffers the first blow.

"From the information on the Russian and Chinese computers, I was stunned to learn none of the three individuals knew the targets being attacked until three hours before the actual attacks began. They complain about a person named Hickler not trusting them with the vital information for security reasons. Apparently, this person— Hickler—controls all the details of the attacks."

Willi took a seat next to Chasey, feeling more secure based on the earlier unsuccessful attempt on his life.

"I would now like to turn the meeting over to Donna. She has a better understanding of the terrain where the past attacks took place."

Donna had not changed clothes since the hospital attack; the small red blood spots on her slacks added to the dangerous atmosphere.

"Being a Native American gives me a better understanding of the land and the relative importance of each attack to date. The first attacks in each country centered on remote homes or sites with very limited deaths. The second wave of attacks caused a larger number of deaths confined to rural areas.

"My best analysis of the impending attacks would be on substantially larger groups of people in urban areas to create a heightened sense of urgency and fear. If there is a method of tracking events in China, that would be the place to start. We can make an educated guess once the planes Willi is tracking have landed.

"I don't know the proper protocol, but alerting personnel who can spot irregular movement or activity in China should be our highest priority. We have limited time—in the past, just eight hours—to respond after China is attacked." Donna raised her voice to stress *respond*.

Colonel MadMan Diana rose quickly from his chair.

"I have worked closely with Willi and Donna for the past month. I believe they have isolated the key points in our search. If I were to predict the area of the next attacks, they would highlight large cities near major government complexes. As much as I hate saying this, my thinking is it will involve large groups of young people. Nothing shouts catastrophe louder than hundreds of dead or injured children.

"In this country, my first scouting report would center on large groups of children congregated near D.C. Ashley has to get permission for us to have helicopter and land surveillance in a hundred-mile radius from ground zero, Washington D.C. The best information we can send to law enforcement is for them to identify similar groups of young people meeting near their capital cities.

"This is my best estimate, which I have discussed at length with Donna and Willi. They agreed—with the limited degree of information available—that the recommendations we developed are the best available."

MadMan ended his remarks still standing next to the circles he had drawn, highlighting what he considered the most likely targets in the U.S.

Hull turned to Ashley. "Do you have any contacts in China that could make us aware of a large attack on one of their cities? The timing of the attack would provide us with enough lead time to stop or lessen the damage in this country."

"None that I would trust," Ashley replied. "Why not ask John Tsia? I trust him. He has been a great team member since joining us. I can clear him into one of our secure comm rooms where he could teleconference with members of his party. The only other option is to have *you* contact your resources—since they asked for you by name."

"You can coach John on what questions to ask without compromising our security. He must be nearby. Can you give him the proper credentials he needs to use this nation's super-secure network?" Hull asked.

"If they won't allow me to work with John, I have an open link to my boss. I am certain once they speak with him—if necessary—there won't be any delays. Tell John to meet me at the exit in twenty minutes. In the interim, you can help me phrase the questions you want to be asked."

John Ashley and John Tsia had no difficulty gaining access to the communications center. The President had removed all obstacles before they could be raised.

Speaking to one of his team members, John Tsia's face showed shock from the conversation he had just held.

"A major political youth rally near our capital has been attacked within the last thirty minutes. My friend told me his unit is providing security for the survivors and will call me when he has more information." Tsia's face alarmed Ashley. Pure rage fired from Tsia's eyes. "My son and daughter are members of the youth group that was attacked." His eyes welled with tears as he spoke to Ashley.

MadMan told Tsia to remain on the call with his friend, hoping to gain more information on the attack. Knowing time was critical, he gathered his notes and ran back to the planning center.

The remaining members of the group were gathered around the conference table, reviewing information on the types of events Donna had described. Chasey was the first to notice MadMan's return.

"That was quick. You haven't been gone more than thirty minutes."

"A large Chinese youth group was attacked within the last two hours." MadMan was breathing hard from running to the meeting room. "If Donna's calculations are correct, Russia will have a similar incident within the next six hours. We must have Jaz contact her superiors with a warning of what to expect."

Colonel Thrasher opened the conference room door, almost running over Chasey, who was on his way to alert Jaz.

"Mr. Hull, you requested I report immediately any and all strange activity throughout Russia and this country. We just received word that a large youth soccer tournament was subject to an attack within the last thirty minutes."

42

Too Little Too Late

Andrews Air Force Base

Top Secret Mission Control Center

2300 Hundred hours

Colonel Brad Thrasher wasted no time with introductions. "John Ashley directed me to assess any and all abnormal activity in areas close to government centers in China.

At 2300 hours, our time, we detected a fleet of small aircraft—most likely drones—descending on a large group of individuals assembled in smaller clusters on what I believe were soccer fields. Our satellite captured many individuals lying flat on the ground. Unfortunately, I could not obtain higher-resolution images of what may have happened.

Ashley requested our scans be limited to areas within an hour's drive from major population centers. This activity took place forty kilometers from Beijing, the capital. In fifteen minutes, I'll be in a position to offer greater detail on exactly what is happening."

Hull and MadMan looked at each other with dismay. What Willi had forecasted was becoming a tragic reality before their eyes.

"Colonel, could we use the rear part of this room to discuss what alternatives are available to our group?" MadMan asked politely, knowing Thrasher's positive response was likely. "We would still be close enough for you to give us new information as you receive it."

Thrasher laughed. "When the big man gives you an order, there's no option but to obey. You're the first and only civilians I know who've set foot in this room. My good nature ends if any of you expect me to make your coffee. I'll stay close, listening on my headset for any new information."

Gathered around a conference table, MadMan spoke first.

"Willi and Donna think the next attack will be centered on a Russian location, similar to what China just experienced. Roy, you have contacts with the military. You should contact them."

"Better if Jaz speaks with them," Hull replied. "We must remain here to evaluate the options available to us. I propose breaking into small teams. There are multiple areas of possible interest based on Willi's calculations.

Donna, John Tsia, and I will form the team for Anacostia Park, where a little league playoff is being played on multiple fields. Our data shows this site is the most likely to be attacked.

MadMan, Jaz, and Peters will cover the second site in Rock Creek Park. A Boy Scout jamboree is scheduled there all day.

Ashley, Chasey, and Blake will stay on the tarmac in full gear, attempting to cover threats we have not yet identified.

Tamara and Willi will remain here to serve as coordinators for any information we uncover.

Time is on our side, as the next attack is expected to occur four and a half hours from now on Russian soil. Jaz can provide them info on the timing of their attack."

Hull spoke deliberately, leaving no doubt about who would be responsible for which area. All the faces around the conference table nodded in agreement while reviewing the notes they had written.

The conference room door burst open, and Jaz entered.

"Your information is flawed," she said, throwing her notes toward Hull. Tears were clearly flowing down her face.

She raised her voice. "I screamed when I spoke with my superiors. There *has* been an attack—on a children's music festival in the small town of Sergiev Posad, which is very close to Moscow. The town was hosting a two-day showcase for young musicians.

They haven't counted individual deaths yet, but their estimate is in excess of one thousand children and adults. People who weren't targeted confirmed a team dressed in safety clothing prevented attempts to help the dying victims—often using automatic weapons to keep people away."

"I have ordered transportation as needed," John Ashley stood up and addressed the group, knowing the urgency of their next steps. "I've reserved short- and long-distance transport with trained crews standing by. When I described what we're facing with our unknown adversary, it was difficult to be more specific about what we'll need and when.

The good news is, all the resources we need have volunteered to help us. From what Jaz reported, our window of opportunity is closing fast. Roy, we need to gear up and assemble without delay."

Kim Hickler's Communication Headquarters

Bhia Blanca Argentina

"Herr Kessler, what can you report on the devastation exacted on our Chinese target, the town of Jiaxing? We selected this site only because it is close to the Chinese capital, Beijing."

"My first reports are even better than Braun and I had planned. My on-site team tells me more than one thousand individuals are dying or already dead," Kessler replied, smiling. He could not hide his obvious delight in their plan working better than expected.

"Excellent. These actions will accelerate the defense funding allocated to our friends." Kim Hickler was anxious to hear additional good news. "Braun, what good news do you have for me?"

Braun, seated next to Kessler, was reviewing the information he had just received.

"My information is not yet as complete as Kessler's. Our attack occurred while my observers were still working to provide me with an accurate count. I can safely say that the Russian attack has created more fatalities than Kessler's. How many more, I'll be better able to tell you in an hour."

As he sat down, he bumped fists with Kessler.

"Now we wait for the fun to begin in the United States. Our trusted agent will contact me directly after the attack."

Hickler, too, could not hide her joy—especially at the large bonus she had earned today.

43

Just in Time

Andrews Air Force Base

Helicopter Staging Area

0900 Hours

Ashley was on the tarmac, speaking to Hull's group gathered around their transportation.

"I called in some favors. After hearing what Jaz told us about what happened in Russia, I decided a normal helicopter wouldn't provide the firepower you may need. You'll be flying in the latest U.S. Army attack helicopter—the AH-64 Apache. It was headed to its home base after receiving all the latest upgrades, complete with a full crew. It took no persuasion on my part to convince the commanding officer to let us borrow the machine and crew for our mission. If there's an attempt to murder thousands of innocents, I wanted something that might change people's minds."

"I don't know how to thank you." Hull grasped Ashley's hand. "If we do need this type of backup, you'd better have additional units standing in reserve. Okay?"

Hull motioned to John Tsia, Donna, and Chasey that it was time to get the show on the road.

The young crew chief made sure all passengers were properly secured with makeshift rigging.

"These craft aren't built for passengers," he laughed, "but you should be safe. The ride shouldn't take more than thirty minutes max. Mr. Hull, the captain would like to see you in the cockpit area."

Hull undid his harness and followed the crew chief. The name tag read **Captain Clemens**, who wore standard reflective sunglasses as the commanding officer. Extending his hand, he shook Hull's firmly.

"I always wanted to meet a distinguished veteran like yourself. When we received orders to divert our trip and proceed to Andrews, I had time to do some online research on the person who could change my flight status. I learned plenty, Major Hull. Your military record speaks for itself."

"What can you tell me, if anything, about the dangers we may encounter?"

"The only information I have is that thousands of people in China and Russia have died this morning from an unknown source. We believe the area you're flying us into has the potential for the same fate—affecting both adults and children. My team believes one of the likely targets today is a three-state youth tennis tournament.

The problem is we have no advanced knowledge—just a sophisticated guess.

"Once my people are off your craft, I'd ask you to circle the area. If possible, I want to break the crowd into much smaller groups. Smaller groups will allow my team to space them out in protected areas. According to the schedule online, the first matches began at 0800 hours. The largest crowds will start arriving around 1100. My team thinks it's best to be prepared."

Hull's voice lacked its usual confidence. "Roger that. Understood. ETA is ten minutes. I'll return to my crew. If I notice unusual activity, I'll alert you immediately. Have us on the ground as soon as possible. Land in any area that provides adequate clearance and security."

Clemens began giving orders to his crew.

"I'm giving John a hazmat suit to wear," Donna whispered to Hull as he regained his seat. "If trouble arises, John has biohazard training from his unit. Not knowing what we're walking into makes me feel unprepared."

The team's discussion came to an immediate halt when the crew chief asked Hull to return to the cockpit—this time without explanation.

Clemens turned to Hull. "You must see this with your own eyes. Look to the left."

Hull followed his gaze.

"I can clearly see hundreds of drones. Nothing is showing up on my instrument cluster. What alarms me most are—what I think are—dead bodies on the tennis courts and in the stands. The drones are flying over the area, appearing to search for more victims."

"How close to the tennis area can you land?" Hull asked. "Two of my people may be able to help the victims on the ground." Hull was certain this was the beginning of the catastrophe everyone feared.

"Can you identify any vehicles? My friend and I will check each vehicle. Past intelligence mentioned a crew preventing anyone from helping."

"Can do!" Clemens replied. "If the drones are responsible for injuring or killing people, would you have any problem if I use the latest laser upgrade recently installed? If I can see them, my weapons specialist can eliminate them."

"No. Your first priority is to warn others who may be arriving. Radio the other helicopter—tell them to fly a circular pattern fifty miles in each direction from the tennis courts. There has to be a drone launch site," Hull replied emphatically.

"We've found the problem area and are landing soon. Donna, you must find the cause of death. John will protect you. There are guards stationed in the hazard area. Chasey and I will scout the same area. The guards must have transportation. Once we find it, they won't be using it."

The prop wash from the departing chopper kicked up earth, leaves, and sand. Clearing his vision, Chasey grabbed Hull's arm.

"There are dark-colored vehicles hidden in a large grove of bushes about one hundred yards east of the courts. Should we escort Donna and John to the court area or hunt for the vehicles?"

Hull turned to ask Donna—only to see she and John already on the courts, kneeling over the bodies.

"Typical Donna," he smiled.

John Tsia followed Hull's instruction to protect Donna, but he hadn't realized how fast she was. He estimated she was fifty yards ahead of him, already kneeling and examining an inert body.

His concern escalated rapidly, causing his heart to pound. Unseen by Donna, two white-clad individuals were running toward her. One held a large, curved knife and was only three steps away, just as Donna was focused on removing something from the victim's mouth and placing it in a sealed plastic container.

Running at full speed, John closed the distance just as the attacker reached for Donna's neck.

Donna became aware of the threat when a strong arm wrapped around her. She saw the knife coming dangerously close—only to watch it fall harmlessly beside her. She couldn't explain why she wasn't killed, until she saw a shooting star embedded in her attacker's right eye, joined by another protruding from his throat.

John reached her. "There are a few more guards coming. Stay behind me. I have my Pit Viper ready. They're armed. I suggest we move toward the bleachers—they'll give us some protection."

"Nonsense," Donna replied. "I have my weapon attached to my side—standard Roy Hull protocol. Let them come. I haven't shot anyone in days."

Hull followed Chasey to the grove of bushes concealing two large vans from view of the courts. Silently, both men crouched to remain unseen. Instinctively, they reached for the bladed weapons they carried—Chasey, his favorite SEAL blade; Hull, the sword he always kept strapped behind his neck.

Chasey pointed to the van closest to them.

"I'll take that one. Circle around and neutralize anyone in the second."

Hull nodded and moved quietly.

Chasey saw the driver's window was open. Crawling on his stomach to avoid detection, he reached the driver's door and gripped the handle. *All or nothing,* he thought, hoping to catch anyone inside off guard. If the door didn't open, surprise would be lost—but at least the people inside wouldn't know who was outside.

Taking a path that allowed him to see without being seen, Hull observed two men speaking into a microphone. He listened closely—they were reporting the attack's status. When he heard that fewer than one hundred had died so far, and listened to them laugh at the suffering of the victims, something primal took over.

He rushed to the van and flung the door open. His blade drove straight into the speaker's throat, blood spurting throughout the van. The man collapsed without a sound. The second man froze, stunned. As he reached for his weapon, the same blade that had killed his partner plunged toward him.

Hull and Chasey regrouped, each scanning for additional threats. Finding none, they turned their attention to Donna and John, who were both crouched in firing stances—low to the ground, weapons ready.

Chasey remarked, "Are my eyes deceiving me, or do I see white-clad bodies riddled with bullets?"

"You go to them," Hull told him. "I'll contact Clemens to pick us up. The police are arriving in force. I'll meet you before they ask too many questions. I have the radios and cell phones those two were using. Willi needs to tear them apart to find out who's behind these attacks."

44

Death Saved

Bahia Blanca Argentna

Kim Hickler's Complex

1700 hours

There must be some communication problem with the team from the United States. I received their initial report at 1600 hours, which is 1000 hours in Washington. I've heard nothing since. The group leader mentioned a small crowd was in the immediate area, but he could see much larger groups entering the complex. They will be walking into a death trap.

Kessler was unsure if the news would please Hickler, who was not in the room.

"Permit me to control the console?" Braun asked as he moved next to Kessler. "I have encountered radio difficulties in the past. Usually, the other operator has changed the frequency by mistake."

Braun's fingertips danced over the control panel. He stopped instantaneously when he heard an American voice. His mind was puzzled by what had happened. The only words he could understand—due to the muffled speech—were that Donna had evidence of what had happened and needed to rush back to her laboratory. She needed her instruments to diagnose exactly what was causing the painful death of the victims.

He carefully wrote what he had heard on the screen log sheet.

"I doubt if our American contacts will continue. They have been eliminated," Braun spoke quietly, not wanting to believe what he had heard.

Braun stared intently at Kessler just as Hickler entered the room.

"We have some bad news to report," both men spoke in unison to bolster their courage.

"Does your bad news correspond to what my American spy just related to me? Our American mission was compromised? An American military helicopter carrying four people and the crew arrived on the scene immediately after our first attack. What I learned is that our audio and visual contacts were lost, plus several of our on-site protective forces were injured or killed. The others surrendered, which is no problem since they knew truly little or nothing at all. It is a setback. We can always find new recruits willing to sell out their country. What more do you have to tell me?"

Hickler's voice was almost silent, but her icy blue eyes sent daggers through both men.

"I recorded a conversation on the radio used by the American team. Somehow, it is now in the possession of our equipment. A person named Donna was in charge of examining the evidence taken from the designated attack area," Braun said to Hickler, while Kessler stood rigidly next to him.

***

Andrews Air Force Base

Apache Helicopters – Designated Area

1500 Hours

Captain Cameron, his tinted glasses removed, spoke to Hull privately.

"My team followed your orders. I dispersed the crowd and canceled the tournament for two days. Seeing the dead bodies made our job painful, but it was easier to explain. As we lifted off to continue patrolling, my weapons officer pointed out a few drones still circling. I climbed above them, and my sharpshooting crew chief used his M4 to bring nine or ten down. We were careful not to endanger people on the ground. Like a good retriever, my team tracked where they fell to earth. We landed, and I have them for you to examine in this duffel bag."

"Given what happened earlier today, these could prove invaluable for our research. Your men certainly have a round or two coming at my expense." Hull shook Cameron's hand.

Donna joined the two men.

"Is this a private conversation? I need to take what I collected back to my lab at the hospital." Her eyes revealed she had been crying. "I examined—but could not save—some children, some as young as one, whose only crime was watching their older brothers or sisters play tennis. My work won't end until I find out exactly what is killing all these individuals.

"My only problem is that the hospital now has several police officers on-site after the attack yesterday, but I need more to guard my assistants and myself during our research efforts. MadMan's team hasn't returned. Chasey and John are watching Willi work his magic on the radio you captured. Based on what happened earlier at the hospital, I need you, Roy, to watch over me while I work."

"Excuse me, Donna, is it? My name is Mitch Cameron, team leader and captain of this helicopter gunship. My crew are all expert marksmen, and to be honest, what we witnessed today caused the hackles to rise on our scalps. Let me have our copter serviced, and my men and I will be happy to escort you. If needed, when the second copter returns, I'll alert their captain to meet us at your hospital."

"Roy, that is an offer I cannot refuse." Donna looked at Hull, her good friend for many years, to make sure he wasn't unhappy with the change.

"Captain Cameron, take care of my best friend. I have to visit my technical wizard to plan our next actions." He kissed Donna lightly on the cheek. "Remember: 'I kill them, you skin them,'" he added, quoting the refrain they had used since their early teens, when trapping animals for their fur—an experience common among Native Americans growing up in Montana.

"Roger that," Cameron shouted at the rapidly disappearing Hull. "Doctor Deer, would you care to join me for breakfast while my machine is being readied for our next mission?"

***

Ascending two steps at a time, Hull felt energized. Although he couldn't stop the slaughter of the first wave of tennis players and fans, he knew his team had saved hundreds—if not thousands—of innocent lives.

Approaching Willi's work area, he had to stop. Chasey and John were exchanging high-fives with Willi. It reminded Hull of the reception he had received at the Naval Academy during his football career.

Chasey acknowledged Hull's arrival.

"Willi is a genuine genius. Using the radio frequencies as a guide, he has positively identified two of the three men responsible for the mass murders. The Russian and Chinese individuals have fictitious names. Willi took it as a special challenge to uncover their actual names. Better to have Willi explain what he accomplished. His skill level is something I've never seen."

Willi rubbed his hands together like a pianist ready to play a Bach etude. Selecting each key with precision, he entered the first frequency he had discovered. The radio emitted a string of notes and then went silent. Hull listened. Chasey listened. Willi stood smiling.

"Once I found the correct frequency from the list glued to the back of the radio, I started in sequential order, hearing a string of sounds that were meaningless. After a few attempts to uncover the intended person or site at the receiving end, I stopped to think.

"What if the sounds were musical notes on a scale? I play the guitar and could recognize different notes. I wrote them down. The notes formed a person's first and last name. The two most-used frequencies displayed a Russian name and a Chinese name. I wrote them down and confirmed not only their names but their locations. It's all written on this sheet. You can use the information at your discretion.

"The individuals sending the information were careless. They apparently never met the two. They needed to be certain the information they sent reached the proper parties. I'd think the people receiving the identifying entry had to respond with a similar code before any future transmissions would follow."

A large smile covered Willi's round face.

"Is there any method you can use to verify the accuracy of your findings?" Hull asked, standing over the radio while looking at Willi's notes.

"Precisely what Chasey and John asked me," Willi responded quickly. "My instincts told me the loss of the radio had not reached the two sites I detected. I entered the first frequency, and we heard a series of notes. I immediately ended the transmission. I repeated with the second and got the same results. The two receiving the radio transmissions are the same two I hacked last week."

"Splendid work, Willi." Hull knew exactly how to use this new information. "I will rely on your notes to give us a competitive edge in bringing them to justice. You stay here. John and Chasey will stay with you for safety. I need to find John Ashley immediately."

Carrying Willi's notes, Hull broke into a slow run as he left.

Bahia Blanca Agrentina

Kim Hickler's Compound

2100 Hours

Kim Hickler sat alone in her private study. The only picture breaking the solid white wall displayed the submarine her grandfather had used to settle in this scenic and bustling town. She smiled while dialing her business associate, Max.

Only a few trusted individuals knew the submarine was sheltered in a secure and remote ocean passageway, camouflaged as a warehouse. Remote cameras monitored the area continuously, capturing all activity in and around the hiding place. Some overly curious locals had breached the locked gates, but Hickler knew her grandfather and father had protected the secret for decades without arousing suspicion from the townspeople. Those who ventured into the forbidden area were always found later—after suffering severe and often deadly injuries. No bodies were ever discovered near the hidden submarine.

She picked up her secure phone and dialed, waiting for a response.

"Max, this is Kim Hickler. We may have a collective problem—one I need you to solve. The medical specialist assigned to the President's investigative team has obtained valuable evidence that could be used to identify our delivery system. Call your mobster friend. Give him strict instructions: the doctor and her associates must be eliminated. Stop at nothing. Tonight."

"We attempted to permanently quiet the good doctor yesterday," Max replied. "One of our covert agents on the President's staff keeps us apprised of her movements. But yesterday, our best efforts not only failed, my local enforcer lost several key men. I was forced to compensate him handsomely for his losses. The cost of a second attempt will have to be shared."

Max was growing weary of spending large sums of money without seeing any return.

"Listen closely to me," Kim said, her voice cold and sharp. She was not used to having her authority questioned. "You will do whatever I tell you. Pay whatever it takes. I want you close to the action—and I expect a live report. Your life depends on it."

Max wiped the perspiration from his forehead. He was in deep trouble and knew firsthand Hickler's reputation for eliminating those who opposed her. Trembling slightly, he picked up his phone and dialed Mishca's private number.

45

Mischa Unhappy

Johns Hopkins Hospital

Main Parking Lot

0400 Hours

Thank you, my friend. Not everyone would drive me at this ridiculous hour. You must be very confident your highly paid mercenaries will finally eliminate the doctor who could cause me great harm. Even though your fees are astronomical, I was not unhappy to pay. The money will be worth it to pacify Hickler. She threatened me with a terrible death if I do not destroy Doctor Deer permanently—and as soon as possible. Max Parris wiped his still-sweating forehead, recalling Hickler's threat.

"What are friends for?" Mischa grinned at his business partner. "When you frantically called me with her threat, I reached out to men who will do anything for money. When I mentioned there would be law enforcement present, they told me money overcomes fear. Many times, their actions are too ruthless. Carnage, even when necessary, can attract unwanted publicity. I mention that only so you understand their tactics are unconventional.

Look out your window. They've just arrived—in the two black panel trucks to our left. Your doctor is about to experience a rather different type of homecoming." Mischa laughed loudly at his joke. "Your informant estimated she should arrive in ten minutes. Nothing better than a well-paid spy."

"Arriving via helicopter, according to his report. Once they land, they can destroy the helicopter with Doctor Deer still inside." Parris reached to wipe his forehead once more. "I admire people who value money over personal safety. It's a quality not often found in intelligent people."

Mischa laughed. "I never said they were intelligent. Money is their only consideration—nothing else. I've been told they have no fear of accepting this assignment, even with law enforcement on the premises. The helicopter carrying the doctor is hovering over the designated landing area. Your fears are ending."

***

"Why aren't we landing?" Donna Running Deer was growing impatient to reach her laboratory and assistants. The evidence she had gathered at the field needed immediate inspection and identification. She and John Tsia had not removed their hazmat gear until her primary air detection equipment confirmed the danger had passed. Yet she could not erase the memory of the dead—their mouths open, eyes gazing into nothingness.

"I would've landed ten minutes ago, but your friend Hull told me to hold position. MadMan is flying a second copter carrying some of Hull's 'special friends.' He instructed me to let them land first," Captain Cameron whispered to Donna. "If he says wait, we wait. You won't have to wait long. I see them approaching behind us.

You'll have two of my crew acting as your bodyguards, since I understand you had some difficulties recently. They've landed. Get ready." Cameron burst into a loud laugh. "You may not even need my men to guard you. The guys with MadMan have a distinctive look. They're all Delta Special Forces—'Snake Eaters,' I believe. Someone with serious power arranged for them to function as your bodyguards. Good luck. And remember, we have a lunch date next week." He rose and opened the copter door for Donna.

***

Max and Mischa were standing outside their vehicle to get a better view of the upcoming action.

"I wasn't informed of a second helicopter. It must be carrying additional medical personnel," Max Parris said, sounding confident—trying to reassure himself.

Mischa muttered an oath. "I doubt the hospital employs Special Forces military. We're close enough for me to see their insignia.

This is bad. I can tell you—they're the most feared and dangerous opponents in any battle."

His cell phone vibrated with an incoming call. "No! I paid you large sums to execute the doctor!" Mischa's face flushed, and the large vein in his forehead protruded with stress.

"Why aren't they attacking?" Parris asked Mischa.

"I don't believe what I'm hearing," Mischa said, exasperated. "Their leader just told me they'll do anything for money—except die. He recognized, as I did, that the doctor has several very professional bodyguards who know how to eliminate threats. They're returning your money, which pleases me not at all."

***

High-Priority Special Communications

Andrews Air Force Base

0500 Hours

"Don't you ever sleep?" John Ashley complained with a grin. "I called in some favors. The network operators are standing by, waiting for your instructions."

"Give them these two contact numbers." Hull handed his notes to Ashley. "I asked John and Jaz last night to use their trusted friends to notify their leaders, asking them to be available at 0600 our time. They told me their leaders agreed. And don't start complaining. The reason you always wear long-sleeved shirts is the tattoo of the coiled snake around a dagger you've got on your left shoulder. A 'snake eater.' I should have known, especially when the President referred to you as 'Special People,' as in Special Forces.

I joined them on missions whenever I took a vacation from the military. No better team to serve with."

A technician approached Ashley. "Both parties you requested are now online. I'll open the links so you can communicate."

Ashley was surprised—but pleased—that the two screens before them displayed the same military leaders he had met earlier this year in the White House special communications office with the President. The scowls on each man's face made it clear this was no casual conversation.

Hull stepped into view. "Generals, you may speak in your native languages. However, I know from experience that you both speak excellent English and French."

Boris, leader of Spetsnaz, spoke first. "There is no language that can convey how badly you have failed our trust. Yesterday, I had the misfortune to attend a mass burial of several young citizens—cut down by the unknown force we both agreed you could prevent. I, for one, feel betrayed and humiliated." His bitterness toward his old comrade could not be mistaken.

General Tsia, leader of the PLA Special Operations, waited patiently for his Russian counterpart to finish.

"I have lost great face with my leaders—and even my subordinates. The mass burial held in the government center reflected poorly on my judgment and my decision to employ you to protect us from whatever evil is descending upon my people." Tsia's face was clouded in disgust.

"Generals, I deserve your scorn," Hull admitted painfully.

"Once I was made aware of the threat to our nations, my actions should have been more decisive. I will not fail you in the future. Permit me to share with you what my team has learned. Three men or organizations—one in each of our countries—have constructed a threat based in Argentina to impose death and destruction on your citizens.

We became aware of the timing once the first attack began in China. The attackers altered their schedule. My team alerted the Russian military, but the warning came too late due to the change in timing. In this country, we were able to prevent the level of deaths you incurred. In the process, my technical team identified the deadly agent and its delivery system. Would you trust me to share this information with you?"

"Of course," Boris replied. "General Tsia and I spoke before this call. Collectively, we have uncovered very little about the agent of death and the delivery system utilized. All we've learned is that people are dying with their mouths open and a painful expression on their faces." Boris's face remained grim and pained. General Tsia nodded in agreement.

"Early this morning, my chief technical specialist—and very close friend—Doctor Donna Running Deer, contacted me with her analysis of the killing agent. She could not believe the results of her original tests on the substance's composition. She called our government's most noted poison gas specialist to confirm her findings. They both agreed the deadly agent had its origins in World War II concentration camps. The gas has been modified into a thin membrane that ruptures on contact. Being semi-hard, it remains effective even in open spaces.

I will send you both samples of what my team has captured, along with their report. We also observed the delivery mechanism: a modern, highly sophisticated drone, manufactured with a rubber coating to shield it from most radar detection. These drones are controlled remotely. My helicopter team knocked several out of the sky. Again, we will send samples and documentation to you."

General Tsia spoke. "It's good that you've uncovered the poison gas and delivery system, but our countries remain vulnerable to further attacks—especially if these drones cannot be detected by radar."

"In our investigation, we uncovered the names of the responsible parties in each country. I suspect the motive behind their actions is greed. My conclusion is that the group is interested only in creating chaos for their own enrichment.

I will list their names so that you can continue your own investigation. The three use a data network we cannot intercept.

However, when the Chinese and Russian operatives use their internet without phone security, we've been able to monitor their conversations without them knowing. The evidence I will present is circumstantial; you must determine guilt or innocence for yourselves. From their conversations, we became aware of a fourth party designated as the provider of the instruments of destruction. Do you want me to continue with their names?" Hull asked the two men.

Both nodded for Hull to proceed.

"Victor Novak is your country's entry into this sophisticated reign of terror," Hull said, turning to Boris. "I believe the data and evidence we're sending will prove helpful."

"General Tsia, does the name Boa Ming sound familiar to you? We have identified him as the Chinese representative."

Hull paused, waiting for Tsia's response.

"Ah yes, I have personal knowledge of Boa Ming," General Tsia replied. "He has a family member high in the ranks of our government. He constantly criticizes our military and promotes his own combat inventions. I have testified several times about the shortcomings of his organization's products.

Currently, I'm aware of his latest offer to our government—high-tech products specifically designed to stop future attacks on our country. I believe the government is in the process of awarding him a substantial contract in response to the recent massacre. No doubt, this tragedy will only increase his influence."

Boris, meanwhile, was searching for his phone. As General Tsia finished speaking, he glanced at the screen and apologized.

"I, too, have a scavenger in our country who picks at the bones of our military budget. Victor Novak and I have crossed paths many times. He's always whispering in the ears of our leaders, claiming his company provides superior equipment compared to our current suppliers. I'm certain my reports have cost him several million rubles in lost contracts.

Within the past six months, his company proposed a system to protect our nation from surprise attacks—without any prior request or need expressed by our government. My nation has suffered a great loss. Even if your evidence is largely circumstantial, General Tsia and I will require more than your data to convince our superiors to take this seriously."

Boris looked directly at Hull.

Hull responded, "Earlier I mentioned that my technical team gained access to the computers of Novak and Ming. I can send you a photograph of Novak, Ming, and an American citizen—Max Parris—dining together at a Paris bistro just prior to the initial attacks. I will send you a copy of that image, along with the data and additional evidence. Draw your own conclusions.

If I am correct, my next request may be to ask for assistance from your special forces in cutting off the head of the snake."

"If your information is sound," said General Tsia with a glimmer of a smile, "my only question would be when—and how many men—you need."

Boris chimed in, "Rest assured, if you need my men, I will be accompanying them. Send the documents via secure transport."

46

Planning for Future

Andrews Air Force Base

Sensitive Compartmental Information Facility

1000 Hours

The base commander was reluctant to permit us to use his most secure area. I pleaded with him, telling him how important our work was—but it had no impact, John Ashley said to the assembled men and women of Hull's team.

"Even Roy Hull couldn't sway the General on the necessity of using this room. I was impressed that not even a hundred-year-old bottle of single malt scotch—retail value easily in the high five figures—could motivate the General. Hull asked if he could use the General's phone, which was graciously allowed. He then pulled a card from his pocket, dialed a number, and waited.

When a voice responded, Hull explained the importance of using a SCIF for our meeting. He handed the phone to the General, who could only stammer, 'Of course, Mr. President,' before handing the phone back to Hull. The General then asked Hull if we wanted coffee and pastries for our meeting."

"What do you propose is our next course of action?" Jaz asked, ever ready to hear what Hull had in mind.

"We must cut the head off the snake," Hull said boldly. "Willi has been listening in and tracking the center of the murderous organization to Bahía Blanca, a port city in Argentina. Within the next twenty-four hours, only those who volunteer will be boarding a chartered plane to that city.

"It's important that you all understand—we will have no government help or assistance if things become dangerous, or even deadly. Our team can only count on each other for support."

"May I offer a revision to your plan?" Agent Peters raised her voice. "Flying in on a chartered plane will arouse suspicion in the minds of any locals remotely connected to the killers. I believe four beautiful women enjoying a vacation in the sun and surf will seem completely normal.

"None of our male team members look anything like vacationers. Your short hair and military bearing would put a bullseye on your back. You'd be better off renting a yacht and anchoring offshore, while we four pleasure-seeking females conduct surveillance in the city."

Hull and Ashley laughed in unison.

"Your plan has considerable merit; I'll grant you that," Hull said, chuckling. "Your evaluation of the situation—and your understanding that local citizens may be aware—does give you four, if all of you volunteer, a great opportunity to see what the city holds for us.

"Unless I hear a better option, start planning your holiday. Each of you will have multiple phones to stay in contact with us. My company regularly schedules yachts for our biggest clients. I'll have them rent us one, which we'll board in Bahía Blanca for a fishing and drinking holiday."

Hull paused, then asked one more question—one he felt was important.

"Why do you think the locals won't be suspicious of you?"

"Short skirts and low blouses," Jaz replied, laughing.

MadMan stood up. "That is the most clever and simple response to a difficult question. I take it we can charge vacation clothes to Uncle Sam?" he said, grinning at Ashley, who only grimaced.

47

Women's Wiles

Luminoso Hotel

Bahia Blanca Argentina

Poolside

10 hundred hours

I could get very used to this life, Donna Running Deer laughed, sipping her coffee. "Tamara should be here to laugh with us. Roy insisted we establish a carefree persona for public appearances. John Ashley is going to turn three shades of purple when he audits our charges—four women searching for a good time."

Jaz, Peters, and Donna looked up as Tamara approached, walking toward them in white linen shorts that accented her long, tanned legs, paired with a black sleeveless blouse.

"Ladies, we're riding in luxury today," she announced. "Having traveled extensively for work, I wasn't about to take no for an answer when the desk manager told me the only rental cars available were old and shabby. So, I called a friend and client—the president of the rental agency—who, bless his heart, is lending us his Mercedes convertible for as long as we need it. He even suggested, and I agreed, that he provide a driver for the morning.

"You need to change clothes for our secret surveillance mission. Hurry up and get dressed."

A few minutes later, the driver greeted them with a polite nod. "Ladies, my name is Carlos. I will be your driver today. My instructions are quite clear: take you wherever you wish to go. Our city offers many interesting and diverse attractions. Would you prefer to visit local churches, museums, art galleries—or perhaps explore the finest in fashionable clothing?"

"Oh no," Jaz laughed, "Carlos, the four of us are on holiday. Just show us places with gourmet food and great entertainment. Where would you suggest four fun-loving women could spend their time?"

Carlos had already guessed what kind of outing they had in mind, judging by their stylish and revealing clothing. The tall woman in the white, skintight shorts was, surprisingly, the most modestly dressed. He silently questioned what line of work they were in. They certainly wouldn't be welcome in most churches.

"There are several favored night spots in town," he replied cautiously. "However, one place I would avoid is called the Rathskeller. It's located near the ocean, in a district called Fuerth. That neighborhood is named after a city in Germany, once a central Nazi air force headquarters. It now serves as the industrial heart of

Bahía Blanca. Strange things have occurred there. People visit and are never seen again. One incident I recall: a man was found hanging out of a window with his throat cut.

"Locals only go there in groups, for safety. If you insist, I can drive through the area as our last stop for photos and shopping. Their shops only deal in clothing for lower-class workers. The Rathskeller is famous throughout Argentina for its superior beef dishes, but I've never had the desire to eat there."

The four women exchanged looks. Fuerth was clearly the site they needed to investigate. There was no doubt in any of their minds. Agent Peters voiced what the others were thinking.

"Carlos, could we visit Fuerth during the daytime? It sounds vastly different from the other places we've seen. The pictures we take there will be a great memento of a momentous day. After that, we'll drive you home."

"No need to return me," Carlos said. "My employer has assigned someone to pick me up."

Carlos drove them through the arched gateway that separated Fuerth from the central part of Bahía Blanca. Each woman discreetly activated her small 3D camera, trained on a pre-assigned quadrant of the complex.

"Carlos, stop at the central plaza," Donna requested. "We need you to take pictures of us—we want to make our friends envious."

"The central plaza separates the two main manufacturing facilities in Fuerth," Carlos explained, his tone flat. "To your left, I'll drive slowly past the chemical processing plant. Only 'special citizens' are permitted to work there, and they must live within Fuerth. You'll notice the large sign at the top of the building warning of death to anyone who enters without authorization.

"To your right is the drone facility, which designs and markets small drones sold online. I own one myself—my son and I have great fun with it. These two plants are the most notable sights in Fuerth.

"Since the day is coming to an end, I can take you back to your hotel or call for my ride. If you'd like to stay, I'll drop you off at the Rathskeller restaurant—you'll beat the dinner crowd."

"Not before you take our pictures," Jaz said as the four women opened the doors of the Mercedes. "First, let us pose in front of the chemical factory."

Carlos laughed uncontrollably as the group contorted themselves into humorous and exaggerated poses. He then waved them toward the drone facility for more antics with that backdrop.

"Enough," he finally said, still smiling. "It's getting late. If you want to stay here, I'll drop you off at the restaurant and call my friend for a ride."

"Before you go," Donna asked, "who lives in that large complex on the edge of town? The architecture is stunning—unlike anything else we've seen."

"I've only heard rumors," Carlos replied, grasping for the right words. "A young woman with an unknown past. I'm told she controls operations at both the chemical and drone facilities. The few times I've seen her, she carries—but does not use—a cane. I've never asked why."

Tamara ended the conversation. "Give me the keys. Call your ride. Would you like a beer at the Rathskeller while you wait?"

"No, thank you. I don't want to go inside. But take care—and stay safe."

Carlos thought silently, *With the way you're dressed, it'll take a miracle for that to happen.*

They waited for Carlos's ride to arrive, then proceeded toward the Rathskeller.

48

Trap is Set

Der Rathseller

Feines Essen Gute Musik

(Fine Dining and Good Music)

Fuerth Bhia Blanca Argentina

2000 Hours

Ladies, remember we are on a fun-seeking holiday, Jaz said, always ready with a quick reminder to the other three women about their cover story. "We have to uncover what this small town holds in manpower, equipment, and facilities."

The four women stepped into the entrance of the restaurant. The odor of cigarette smoke, beer, and the aroma of meat being grilled was heady and filled their senses with a strange feeling—like being in a Gasthaus in Germany.

Immediately upon seeing the women enter, a young blonde hostess dressed in authentic German clothes greeted them. "Welcome to Der Rathskeller. What is your pleasure this evening?"

Peters responded, "The four of us are looking for a great meal and some laughs. Our holiday has been boring. We were told your food is the finest in all of Argentina by our hotel concierge. If we can't find laughter, at least we can enjoy your food."

"If you savor fine food, our chef's special today is *kartoffel und das steak.* Just the scent of the roasting meat should be enough to make you hungry," the blonde hostess said with a smile.

"Sounds just like what we're searching for," Donna replied in fluent German. "*Bier, bitte,* to help wash it down."

"What did you order for us?" Jaz asked. "I'm famished. And where and when did you learn to speak German?"

"When Roy and I were very young, all our teachers came from different countries. We were exposed to a variety of foreign languages. It was mandatory to learn a new language every year as we advanced through school. I know Roy can read and speak a dozen or more languages. He told me once there were at least a dozen he could speak fluently.

"His language proficiency was questioned at the Naval Academy only once. The commandant sat him in a room with twelve language professors. The story his father told me was this: he would be asked a question in one language, and he had to answer in a different second language. Eight hours later, he was excused from taking any future language classes and was asked if he could substitute for a regular instructor if another teacher was unavailable." Donna's response did not seem to surprise the other women.

"Speaking of my husband," Tamara added in a slow, low tone, "Roy sent me a short text. He and the others will be in the marina early tomorrow morning. He believes one or more of us may be in danger of being discovered."

"Your husband worries too much," Jaz laughed. "Each of us is wearing a wig. The only thing any man might notice—other than the two old guys at the bar—is the long legs of Peters in her very short skirt."

A waiter approached their table, followed by the hostess carrying dishes laden with food. He placed them gracefully before each woman. As he turned to leave, Donna held up her hand, indicating they wanted refills on the beer steins.

"If we're on a holiday, best to give the impression of being a little tipsy. Although," she added with a smirk, "there aren't any men in here that look all that interesting."

Five minutes later, a group of ten to twenty younger men poured through the doors. It was clear they had come straight from work, as their uniforms were similar. It didn't take long for them to notice the four scantily dressed women who were laughing and drinking their *bier*. Their laughter was loud and inviting.

Peters spoke in a muffled voice. "I believe our targets for tonight have arrived."

Five minutes later, a band appeared at the back of the room, where a large dance floor was located. The band featured a lead accordion player, backed by a drummer, pianist, and saxophone player.

"That's our cue, ladies," Peters said. "Get up and dance with each other, and keep laughing. Come on, Tamara—let's show the other two how it's done."

The band was playing a disco hit from the seventies. Tamara and Peters, with their long legs and rhythmic moves, caught the eye of every man in the room. When they returned to their table, Jaz and Donna raised their steins in a toast. Donna motioned to the hostess to refill their liquid entertainment.

The band then started playing a much different song. It was fast-paced, with the accordion player standing apart from the others.

"What type of song is that?" Jaz asked with a laugh.

"It's called a polka," Donna answered. "A favorite dance in many European countries."

She had just finished explaining when a man approached their table.

"Hello, my name is Wilhelm. I was wondering if one of you young ladies would do me the honor of dancing with me?"

Jaz, Peters, and Tamara all grinned and shook their heads in unison. "We're honored," they said, "but none of us has ever danced to this kind of music."

Wilhelm smiled politely at the rejection and slowly turned away—until Donna's voice rang out.

"It would be my pleasure to dance with you," she said loudly.

The three women gaped in amazement at the skill and elegance displayed by Donna and Wilhelm. It quickly became apparent that the two were far superior dancers. Other couples gradually left the floor to give them more space to show off their moves.

As the music ended, Wilhelm took Donna's arm and escorted her back to the table.

"I must explain," he said. "I'm a dancing instructor in my idle hours. Your friend Donna is a much better dancer than I am. I'm hoping that wasn't our last dance this evening?"

He turned with a warm smile and returned to his group.

Jaz, Tamara, and Peters silently clapped their hands as Donna sat down. Never one to stay quiet for long, Jaz asked, "Where did you develop the exquisite dancing skills you just displayed?"

The other women leaned forward to hear her answer as the band started up another loud musical piece.

Donna shook her head, laughing as her long hair tossed from side to side.

"Not many people outside our immediate families know Roy and I won several national and international dancing championships in our youth. Roy's parents were champions in the adult category. We won junior championships until we graduated from high school and left for college. I hadn't danced in many years. That and the samba were our signature dance moves."

"Roy can dance?" Tamara raised her voice over the music. "The few times we attended events that offered dancing, he always told me he had never learned. He and his father preferred hunting and trapping, leaving little time for an active social life. Wait until I get him alone."

"Wilheim is the leader of the group wearing red shirts," Donna told her friends. "He proudly informed me his team was named the 'Cleaners.' When I asked what cleaning was needed in this small town, he just smiled at me like I wouldn't understand. When I asked what the men in the blue shirts were called, he smiled again— 'Protectors.' I enjoyed dancing with him, but I think we need to broaden our social circle to learn more—if there's more to know about this town. We seem to be the only women here under sixty."

Wilheim wasted no time when the band started playing a popular rock ballad from the past. He was joined by three men, all sporting red shirts. As Wilheim had done, the men introduced themselves to the women. After the second song began, it became clear the blue shirts had been instructed not to interfere with the arrangement.

Three hours passed. The dancing ended. All of the men left— except for Wilheim, who quickly intercepted Donna before she could leave with her friends.

"Before you go," he said, "I would be honored if I could change your mind about returning later this week. Ladies, if you don't object, I'd like to show you an attraction that I'm certain will pique your interest."

Donna turned to the others.

"I'll be perfectly safe. Wilheim is walking with me to the water's edge. He has a building of interest at the pier. It's within eyesight."

Wilheim took her arm, and the two carried on a conversation, with Donna shaking her head in laughter. The girls overheard her say, "You must be crazy if you thought I would believe that."

Wilheim and Donna stood by the deck railing before he led her down a gangway into the building they had viewed from above. The two returned less than fifteen minutes later.

"I owe you an apology for doubting you," Donna said slowly, giving Wilheim a quick kiss on the cheek. She was still laughing as she went to join her friends.

Tamara started the car while the others bombarded Donna with questions.

"Wait until we return to the hotel," Donna said. "I saw something I can't comprehend. With the information we gained this evening, it needs to be written down."

"I admit my dancing skills aren't as advanced as Donna's, but the majority of my dances have been with Gustavo," Jaz said, laughing as the women changed into something more comfortable and sipped wine provided by room service, courtesy of Tamara. "I don't think my feet will ever be the same." She wrinkled her nose in mock disgust.

"What I did learn was that something extremely important is happening next week. Gustavo acted as though he'd be on duty and unavailable then."

"My hand-to-hand training came in handy while dancing, mostly with Hans," Peters added. "It took every ounce of focus to keep from having my feet trampled. Despite the pain, Hans was very talkative. When I asked if being a Cleaner was demanding, he grinned and said, 'People never expect a surprise when they open their front door.' I couldn't tell if he was joking."

Tamara, having finished writing, joined the conversation.

"My dance partner, Paul, told me how proud he was to be promoted to the Cleaners after completing training as a Brandenburger elite graduate. I made a mental note, since I had no idea what that meant. As a Protector, he said life was dull. He mentioned two names—Kessler and Braun—who required twenty-four-seven protection. Guarding Kessler required them to wear very warm, special clothing, which was uncomfortable. For Braun, ordinary military clothing was enough. He also mentioned a woman named Hickler, who only demanded an escort when traveling outside the complex. He described her as the brains behind whatever their operation is. He said Hickler always carried a cane, even though she didn't need it to walk."

Jaz turned to Donna. "You definitely caught Wilheim's interest—tonight, or maybe longer."

"I had told him we wouldn't be returning to Fürth due to the lack of excitement and because we wanted to visit other towns," Donna replied. "But our trip to the water's edge and that building changed my mind. You won't believe what I saw. I'm still puzzled."

She paused as the others leaned in.

"The building houses a World War II Nazi submarine. Wilheim told me that if we returned, the four of us would be his guests for an ocean voyage with him and the others."

Donna hesitated, seeing the dumbfounded expressions of her friends—just as she had looked when first gazing at the Black Sea monster.

49

Very Strange Craft

Supra Yacht Sales

Bahia Blanca Port

0600 Hours

Pepe Salas grumbled inwardly. He wanted nothing more than to return to his warm bed for another four hours. But that was not his fate. Late last evening, he had received a phone call from a man who made it clear he was not to ask any questions. The instructions were clear and concise.

A large fishing yacht would be tied up at his dock before 0630. His tasks: retrieve the keys placed under his inside mail drop, refuel the vessel, and stock it with drinking water and supplies for eight people.

Pepe had never encountered a vessel constructed quite like this one. It was wider than any craft he had ever seen. The note instructed him to hand over the keys only to a man named *El Loco*. The name alone was enough to unsettle him.

***

"Roy, why do we have to arrive at this harbor town so early?" MadMan asked, still yawning after waking at 0300 and driving for the next three hours.

Hull smiled. "John Ashley called me last night. The police guarding the hospital found pictures of Chasey, Peters, you, and me. Each of the photos was marked with a seven-figure bounty for our deaths. That tells me those images are likely circulating at every site we've stayed at."

He paused, then continued, "Given this town is the central hub of all the organizations being paid to eliminate our group, I figured it was best to travel at night to avoid being recognized. Peters is my main concern since she's in the middle of town, unaware she could be in danger."

"I placed a call to an old Navy buddy and described the kind of vessel we'd need," he added. "He said it would be moored at the local marina. No need to show ID—if the manager asks who I am, I'm supposed to draw my sword."

***

"Where should I stow our gear?" Dan Chasey asked, still rubbing his eyes, groggy from the rapid travel and lack of sleep.

"Place it with the other weapons on board," Hull instructed. "Take an inventory of whatever my friend managed to scrounge up for us. I want to leave in thirty minutes. We've got a lot of scouting to do before planning our next operation. I'm counting on Jaz to provide the information we need."

50

Victory at Last

Wolfhead Headquarters

Munich Germany

1200 Hours

Richard Hickler rose to address his comrades-in-arms of many years.

"I have just been in contact with my daughter," he announced. "She assures me the final attack will occur within the next forty-eight hours."

"Herr Hickler, if your information is correct, we must urgently pass this news to our comrades in other parts of the world," said the aging, small man. "The promise of future greatness is now at hand."

He raised his right arm, holding it straight and proud.

51

Final Plans

Half a mile off of Bahia Blanca

0400 Hours

Hull rose in front of the group. "MadMan, double-check the ordnance we have at our disposal. Once the women give us the sign to board the sub, we can't go back for additional supplies. The rest of you, gather around for assignments."

He paused, then continued, "MadMan and Jaz have formed a plan of action that depends on timing and teamwork. One screw-up after we take control of the submarine and personnel—you can bet we'll never see land again. That's a certainty, not a threat.

"Once we breach their defenses, these are the teams and assignments: Donna and Chasey have the most dangerous mission. They must determine what can be done to negate the threat of the deadly gas. They may need additional resources. Blake, you'll be one of the snipers providing cover to all teams if needed. Should Donna and Chasey require extra assistance, that will be your primary mission.

"MadMan and Peters will secure and set fire to the drone production facilities. Tamara and John will be charged with kidnapping Kessler and getting him back to the sub—alive, preferably. Jaz volunteered to bring Braun back to the submarine, perhaps with injuries if necessary.

"Of course, all plans go off-center once the shooting starts. Each of you has dealt with crisis situations many times. Improvising and eliminating any threats is your only plan of action. Get some rest. If all goes well, we intersect with the sub at 1900 hours."

"Wait, where are you going to be while we're under duress attacking the complex? I never knew you to duck a fight, ever," Chasey said, puzzled. He had experienced several battles—some more dangerous than what was planned.

"I'm going after the head of the snake—Hickler. She is clearly the leader of their operation. If left alive, she could plan and launch another one just like this. I know where her guarded residence is located. If, for some reason, I don't make it back to the sub, carry out the mission as planned." Hull's voice was decisive.

***

Hotel Meeting Room

1100 Hours

"I called Wilheim. He was almost at a loss for words when I told him the four of us would be delighted to enjoy a ride on his submarine. He said he'd call me back in thirty minutes—he needed approval from his superior but mentioned it was just a formality. He just called back and told me approval was granted. I was surprised Wilheim even had a superior—until now, I was led to believe he was the ultimate authority." Donna couldn't hide her laughter.

"Yes," Jaz added, joining in the laughter. "The thought of having four helpless females submerged some distance from shore—he and his friends believe they hold all the advantage when it comes to what they think of as 'payment' for the unique submarine adventure. Remember, Hull needs the submarine fully above water to take control. Practice your best claustrophobic movements. Whatever Hull has planned depends on the sub being accessible."

"Knowing what my husband is capable of, nothing will surprise me," Tamara chuckled. "He rescued me from a sinking yacht with an underwater AUV while people were shooting at us in France. Our task is to completely immobilize the four men acting as our generous hosts."

"Immobilized means death in my country," Jaz interrupted Tamara. "Once the action starts, follow my lead. Hull and I examined what options will be available to us. Donna, you have the most challenging task—persuading Wilheim to turn over control without having to kill him first. As for me, I will relish providing Gustavo with a life-changing experience—just as he's done to others. A fact he's boasted about to me on several occasions.

"If my plan with Hull works as discussed, the rest of you will wait until I come back from my 'gift' to Gustavo before threatening your companions. I will emphasize how serious their cooperation is—without providing any other information. Donna, I repeat, you have the most delicate task: persuading Wilheim to cooperate. He has to notify the engineers to return to shore without question."

"I have the skill and physical knowledge to render pain until he becomes compliant to our commands. Trust me," Donna responded to Jaz without hesitation.

"Agreed. Just be ready to seize the moment when I make my entrance," Jaz said again.

"Wilheim suggested we dress in loose-fitting clothing. He told me dinner at the restaurant is at five, followed by what he described as a 'sailing adventure of a lifetime,'" Donna added with a laugh. "Loose-fitting clothes—meaning easy to remove."

"It's twelve now. I'll notify Hull—our ETA for boarding is approximately 1900 hours. Remember, once on the submarine, wait for my signal before you three go into action," Jaz concluded, ending the conversation.

***

One Half Mile from Bahia Blanca

Small Meeting Room

1300 Hours

"Be careful where you sit. One accidental movement will send this craft—and us—to the moon," Hull warned with a smile. "I just heard from Jaz. Time to review our last-minute assignments for tonight.

"John Tsia and I will be in the water in case the submarine deviates from our plan. We both have deep-water diving training, and John has many hours of submarine experience. We'll use unconventional means to make the sub surface if necessary. However, I'm confident in Jaz's plan to take full control."

"Once we're on board, I'll need all hands to assist me in loading the munitions we're sitting on onto the submarine," Chasey said emphatically. "They are the means of destroying—or rendering ineffective—buildings and materials that pose a threat."

52

Postponement

Hickler Communications Room

0900 Hours

Kim Hickler reviewed the latest refinement added to the planned drone bombardment. She was unhappy with the one-day delay, but Wilheim had explained that producing the necessary quantity of the poison gas was taking far longer than planned.

Making some last-minute notes, she dialed the special encrypted line set up by Max Parris.

"Hickler, so good to hear from you. The three of us spoke yesterday about the timing of your next deadly surprise." Victor Novak was anxious to learn the date when the targeted countries would suffer the consequences of delaying his and his associates' systems—meant to end the terror that had befallen them in the past.

"I purposely called you first. Your payment was five million euros short of what I asked," Kim Hickler said, her voice pure ice, delivering her displeasure without hesitation. "It would be a disservice to your compatriots if I felt it necessary to delay the impending disaster due to your failure to comply with my demands."

Nicely done, she thought to herself, shifting the blame for the delay onto Novak.

"That cannot be accurate!" Novak shouted into the phone, his voice panic-stricken. "Give me an hour to check my records and call you back."

"I will give you thirty minutes. If I do not hear from you in that time, your partners will be notified that the next attack will be delayed—until I receive the full payment, either from you or from them." Hickler terminated the discussion, once again congratulating herself on shifting the blame to Novak.

She had purposely selected Victor. His mind had shown signs of instability during several of their previous face-to-face meetings.

53

Shifting Blame

Kim Hickler Private Communications Room

Bahia Blanca

0800 Hours

Kim Hickler was disturbed by Wilheim's report that the next aerial attack was being delayed by a day—or possibly two. Such a delay would be financially unsatisfactory due to the penalties written into the secret agreements signed by the four of them.

As she examined possible alternatives, her mind quickly targeted Victor Novak. In past meetings, he had exhibited brief periods of mental instability, noticeable to her and the others.

After jotting a few notes to herself, she selected the private encrypted line installed by Max Parris and dialed Victor Novak. The phone rang only once before he answered.

"I was just about to contact you. The three of us are most anxious to hear the date of the attack planned for this week. The vision of hundreds—or thousands—dying in terrible pain will emphasize the crucial need for our unique defensive systems in each of the targeted countries," Novak said quickly, slurring his words.

"Unfortunately, the plans have been delayed. Your latest payment was five million euros short. Before I can authorize the massive attack you're expecting, either you or your friends must make up the shortage," Hickler said bluntly, her tone sharp and unforgiving.

"There must be some kind of mistake! I need time to check with my financial staff. I'll call you back after I confer with them," Novak shrieked, his voice cracking.

Well done, thought Kim. Shifting the blame to Novak would almost certainly be understood by his partners, who would blame him—not her team—for the delay. Even better, she could now justify imposing a penalty for the supposed shortfall, despite knowing full well that Novak had actually paid the correct amount.

54

Change in Plans

World War II

German Submarine

Officer's Private Dining

1830 Hours

Peters was becoming more agitated by the second as Hans's hands grew increasingly invasive. She thought to herself, *I may have to break his arm or neck*—both actions she knew would endanger or possibly end their mission.

Wilheim broke the silence, pulling Donna ever closer to him.

"It appears Gustavo and your friend Jaz have discovered a more pleasant method of staying submerged and out of sight. I recommend the solution for the rest of us. Good champagne with good company equals a most enjoyable journey."

A knock on the door caught the attention of all six, as strict orders had been given to the crew not to disturb the officer's quarters under any circumstances.

"Open the door, Hans. You're closest," Wilheim ordered sternly. "Discipline the insolent crew member who dares disturb us." He was clearly displeased that one of his strictest rules had been disregarded.

Hans opened the door, and all six stared in disbelief. Standing in the doorway was a completely naked Gustavo. Their initial shock deepened when they noticed a gaping wound in his forehead, blood still streaming from it. Moments later, his body hit the floor face-down, revealing shattered parts of his skull.

He had been shoved forcibly by Jaz, who stood behind him dressed in camouflage military gear. A semi-automatic rifle was draped across her shoulders, a pistol ready in her hand, and a knife strapped to her thigh.

"Sorry to interrupt your party," Jaz shouted, ensuring no misunderstanding, "but the ladies and I are on a mission." She pointed her revolver at Wilheim's head as she walked closer. "I need you to order the captain and the engineer to meet us here. We need this submarine on top of the water—immediately."

Wilheim turned pale as the blood drained from his face. "It is strictly forbidden for us to surface so close to land."

"My dear Wilheim," Donna whispered, "we suspected there might be a problem. Each of us took precautions to defend ourselves. Should you not obey Jaz's commands, I have my sharpest surgical scalpel in my right hand. I can have you singing soprano in seconds, since your body was clearly prepared for a different kind of pleasure."

She leaned in closer. "You will endure immense pain. Depending on your cooperation, I may leave you in that physical state. But if Jaz deems it necessary, I may slice your carotid artery and leave you bleeding to death within seconds. The choice is yours."

Wilheim felt Donna's hands unbuttoning his already loosened slacks.

"Hand me the phone, please," he said to Hans. Then he spoke into it: "Kurt, this is Wilheim. I need you and Engineer Adam to come to the officers' stateroom immediately. We have a slight change of plans."

Wilheim had calculated that the intruders knew nothing about the security force stationed in separate quarters—personnel whose orders were to repel any and all intruders by any means necessary. These were plans laid decades ago, and still in effect.

Jaz looked at Peters. "After the two crew members arrive, take Hans and Paul below. Handcuff them to a bulkhead. Whether they live or die is completely up to you."

"With pleasure," Peters replied with a grin. "Handsy Hans will have a lot of begging to do." She laughed out loud.

No more than five minutes later, a sharp knock on the door signaled the arrival of the two crew members. Jaz stood behind the door as it opened.

The two men stood in the doorway, struggling to comprehend the mutilated body of their friend, Gustavo, lying before them.

"Step over his body," Jaz directed, stepping out from behind the door, "but keep his image in your mind. If you do not obey my instructions exactly, your body will join his."

Both men complied, their gazes fixed on Gustavo as they gingerly stepped over him.

"Wilheim, what is happening?" asked Kurt, wearing the captain's uniform, his voice muffled with fear.

Wilheim, now visibly perspiring, responded haltingly. "As you see, we were deceived by these women and are now their captives. Do whatever they command. Trust in our strong defenses to defeat whatever they have planned."

"You heard your leader," Jaz said, leaning close and whispering loudly into Adam's ear so everyone could hear. "Do exactly what I tell you. I need this submarine surfaced and stopped—immediately. One of these women will accompany you and remain in direct contact with me. Should I not hear from her, you can say goodbye to Wilheim as you leave."

Adam blurted, "Wilheim, we've been taught for years never to expose our vessel to the township. I cannot obey her order!"

"Look down at Gustavo. Captain, move to your left," Jaz said, her voice cold. "I'll only ask you once, Adam. Your options are to obey my orders—or die."

Adam looked to Wilheim, then Kurt. Their blank, disbelieving eyes offered no guidance. Seeing no other option, he replied, "I do not want to end up like Gustavo. I'll bring the vessel to a complete stop as soon as we're above water, just as you directed."

"Tamara, stay with them," Jaz instructed. "I'll stay in contact with you."

"Gentlemen, take one last look at Gustavo," Jaz commanded.

55

Boarded

Atlantic Ocean

500 meters from Bahia Blanca

Depth 80 meters

1900 Hours

Protected by hundreds of hours of special training and the most advanced scuba equipment, Hull and John maintained a vigilant search for the XXI Nazi submarine. Its distinctive shape and technology were far superior to any other WWII submarines.

John tapped Hull on the shoulder. A dark shape, much like a prehistoric monster, came into their clouded sight. They had purposely given the area Jaz had calculated a wide berth, remembering the phrase: *"A submarine coming to surface has little control on where it eventually breaks water."*

Hull and John waited patiently for the submarine to reach the surface before swimming toward it. Locating the maintenance footholds, both men shed their protective eyewear and proceeded to navigate the perilous climb to the deck area. Once secure, they withdrew their machine pistols, not knowing the number or type of protective forces the submarine might hold ready for them.

Slowly, the hatch opened, permitting occupants to emerge onto the open deck. Weapons ready, John and Hull waited for the first person to exit. A fully clothed seaman tumbled down heavily from the opening, landing on his back. He remained in a fetal position, shrieking, *"Diese Schlampe ist verrückt!"*

The next seven men all shouted much the same. Hull, laughing, translated for John, "That bitch is crazy."

Last to climb down was Jaz, her revolver pointed directly at the man who preceded her.

"Peters and I knew there had to be a unit whose only mission was to defend the vessel. Finding the location was the problem. Peters noticed a compartment with no name—only a swastika. I knocked on the door. The man who answered attempted to warn the others. My revolver filled his mouth, making him speechless. I told the rest that if they didn't heed my instructions fast, I would pull the trigger to emphasize my point. That made the unit more eager to listen to what I wanted. Works every time," Jaz added.

"Perfect timing," Hull said, taking out his infrared flashlight and waving it above his head. The signal was invisible to the human eye. Within seconds, the boat lights switched on and moved toward the submarine.

"Give me a hand tying up!" Chasey's booming voice broke the evening silence. "We've got over five hundred pounds of ordnance to unload to your sub."

Hull turned to Jaz. "Keep your revolver handy while demanding the protective crew move the ordnance to the submarine. Place it in their living quarters with Peters as a guard. The unloading and return trip shouldn't take more than sixty minutes. We have a strict schedule to maintain."

Jaz smiled, issuing orders in German while recklessly waving her revolver in their faces. Though still muttering the phrase about her mental condition, the men didn't hesitate to unload and reload at record speed.

"Blake and I will stay with you into port. I told the captain to take it back to shore, refuel it, add provisions, and not let anyone near this boat. Period," Chasey reported to Hull.

"Need all hands on deck. Welcome aboard." Hull shook hands with Chasey and Blake. "Keep your weapons ready. The next hour is the most dangerous. This submarine has to enter its docking quarters submerged. The degree of cooperation is suspect. Any doubt about how to act—follow Jaz's lead. She gets results."

"Kurt and Adam obeyed all of my directions coming into port," Tamara reported to her husband. "They're presently tied to the bulkhead door with blindfolds and gags. Time for me to ready myself for kidnapping Kessler."

"The crew and Wilheim's friends are all secured in various compartments," Jaz confirmed.

"Good. Time to review our plans one final time." Hull gestured to his team to gather around the circular table for his final briefing.

"Speaking to each of you individually and within your teams, it became evident my original plans were inadequate to achieve our goals of eliminating the drone production facilities and the poison gas laboratory. The only person with the required knowledge is Kessler, the lead chemist.

"Tamara and John, before we can initiate any other actions, you two have to bring Kessler here for the technical information only he possesses. Once he's here, you'll have a short window to extract the information Donna needs to render the chemicals useless. You two should leave now. Be careful—and check your weapons."

"To the rest of you," he continued, "give Tamara and John thirty minutes before you take your positions. Peters and Madman need to create a diversion before Donna and Chasey can seize the moment to enter the poison lab. They have no idea what state the gas is in or how to transport it safely."

Hull walked rapidly to say goodbye to his wife.

"Don't you worry, dear husband," Tamara smiled to reassure him. "This is many times more thrilling than investment charts."

"This action may not be as challenging as your past exploits," she added with a wink. "When I tell the story, some may wonder what *you* do to merit such an active wife protecting *you*."

56

Kessler

Outside of Kessler Residence

1930 Hours

The house looks unguarded, John spoke softly to Tamara. "You stay here. I'm going to check the back of the house. I'll text you if I uncover anything. Keep your weapon handy. The new pistol has an active shot suppressor."

John crept carefully, testing for any sensors guarding the home against intruders. He had only traveled fifty yards when he heard the sounds of an attacking dog coming from the area he had just vacated.

Wasting no time, he backtracked quickly as Tamara was shouting for help. A large German Shepherd had attacked her from behind.

The dog's owner kept shouting, "Töten! Töten! Töten!" (*Kill! Kill! Kill!*) as the animal tried to bite through Tamara's arm, which she was using to protect her throat.

The two forms were so entangled that taking a shot was too risky. John reached into his pocket for a throwing star. With a flick of his wrist, the beast rose to confront him. Another flick, and the dog fell silent with a loud groan.

Tamara scrambled to her feet, frantically searching for her revolver. The dog's owner stood silently, leash in hand, stunned and confused by what had taken down his beast so swiftly and silently.

In fury, the man lashed out at Tamara with the leash. Another flick of John's wrist brought the man crashing to the ground, clutching his right knee and screaming in pain.

Tamara pointed her revolver directly at his face. "We're here to see Kessler."

"Nein! Nein! Ich bin Kessler! I speak English! What do you want with me? I'm just a simple chemist in our pesticide manufacturing facility," he groaned through the pain.

"We know your pesticides are designed to murder people. You have the knowledge to stop this mayhem," Tamara said coldly. "We need the information on what chemicals are ready for use—and, more importantly, how to dispose of the finished product."

"Take me inside my home! Hickler will have me killed if I give you what you ask for. The pain in my knee is killing me!" Kessler screamed, pleading for relief.

"I will have John throw more darts into other parts of your body. Then I'll order him to enter your home and kill your wife and daughter," Tamara shouted directly into his face, spittle flying from her mouth.

Moments later, the porch light flicked on, illuminating the area where Kessler and Tamara stood. A blonde-haired woman and a small girl clutching a doll emerged from the house.

A brilliant idea flashed into Tamara's mind. Expecting Kessler would rather die than help them, she leaned in. "Tell your daughter to hold her doll over her head."

Kessler, still in pain, said, "Kristen, my sweet, please hold your doll over your head for me."

The small girl stared in confusion at her mother. The woman, puzzled but understanding—seeing her husband on the ground and a woman pointing a large revolver at his head—repeated the command.

The girl obeyed, raising the doll high over her head. Tamara nodded to John. In one swift motion, he threw another star. The doll flew from the girl's hands and came to a violent stop, its head still vibrating, pinned to the doorframe.

John ripped a piece of Kessler's shirt to stop the bleeding, removed the throwing star, and used the torn fabric as a makeshift tourniquet. Helping Kessler to his feet, he supported him to their car.

Tamara walked briskly back after a brief visit with Kessler's trembling wife and daughter on the lit porch.

"I warned her not to alert the authorities. Her husband's life depends on her silence. John, drive to the meeting place where Donna and Chasey are waiting. We're far behind schedule. Rather than take time to return to the submarine, Kessler will be more helpful at his factory."

Der Rosenkavalier Gasthuas

Fuerth Argentina

2000 Hours

Braun sat sipping slowly from his heavily decorated stein. By this time in the evening, his handsome features—combined with his wavy blond hair—usually drew one or more women to sit beside him, engaging in small talk until he suggested a more secluded rendezvous in the upstairs apartment he rented.

Little did Braun know that outside the Gasthaus, a woman dressed in combat fatigues was stopping all women under fifty from entering. She was offering money and, more importantly, free drink coupons for another venue within a mile. Those who hesitated quickly changed their minds when she withdrew a long blade from its sheath. Presented with the alternative, everyone accepted Jaz's "generosity."

Inside, a waitress approached Braun and discreetly placed a note on his table. Bored and curious, Braun opened the note, which was decorated with hearts. It read:

"My husband is very jealous. He has many friends here, making it dangerous to see you. I am waiting to visit with you. I have been in love with you since the first time I saw you at the military ball. Please, I beg you, my husband will return in the morning. Step outside for a cigarette. When you light it, I will introduce myself. I've made all the arrangements for a night you will never forget."

A large "J" dotted with roses ended the message. Braun smiled to himself—perhaps the night wasn't a total failure after all. Rising from his table, he stepped into the cool evening air. Placing a cigarette between his lips, he flicked on his lighter and waited for his mysterious admirer.

Cold steel pressed against his neck, sending a chill through him.

"I promised you an evening you'll never forget," Jaz whispered.

Laughing inwardly, Braun felt a mixture of delight and suspense. An admirer with imagination and passion was rare, and thoughts of what might happen soon in his secret apartment deepened his smile.

Then he felt a trickle of blood moving slowly down his neck.

"Enough of this foolishness," he said sharply, suddenly realizing he may have misjudged the situation.

"Keep your mouth shut while I place a gag in it. I've already killed one of your 'Cleaners' tonight. Killing you will double my pleasure if you resist. My orders are to take you back to our headquarters. These handcuffs will make it easier to lead you to my car," Jaz said coldly.

100 Meters Outside the Poison Gas Factory

Fürth, Argentina

2000 Hours

"We brought you a present," Tamara whispered to Donna and Chasey in the back of the van the two had driven to the site. "We have Kessler. In person."

"Can we count on him to give us the essential information we need?" Donna asked. "Chasey and I have reviewed the most likely places the poison gas could be stored, but it's just an educated guess. One mistake and Dan and I are history. Now we wait for Peters and MadMan to create the diversion before we act."

"I'm certain he'll cooperate." Tamara held up the doll with the shooting star buried deep in its forehead and showed it to Kessler. "He speaks English and understands the consequences of not assisting us."

"Have him stand between Chasey and me," Donna ordered. "We need very detailed information on the exact location of the poison gas ready for use." She looked directly at Kessler to be sure he understood.

"Yes, it is very dangerous," Kessler replied. "Only Hickler and I have the code to unlock the freezer holding the gas. Once unlocked, the gas is placed into special containers for attachment to the drones. Follow in my footsteps precisely—this area is heavily mined."

Kessler limped noticeably, taking extreme caution. One wrong step could mean instant death for both him and Chasey. Pointing to a clearing, he said, "Stay here. This area is safe."

Tamara and John nodded in understanding. Donna looked at Chasey. "I'm entering the building with him."

Kessler, Chasey, and Donna moved carefully toward a door. Kessler entered a code, then immediately placed his eye on a scanner for additional security. Chasey, revolver drawn, entered first, followed by Kessler and Donna.

Kessler led them to another closed door. "I must warn you, there's a timer on the freezer. You have ten minutes to extract the containers before security arrives. There should be two containers, each weighing ten kilos."

Donna held her finger to her lips. "What about the substances not in the freezer?"

Kessler whispered, "The gas isn't lethal until I add the final component. That was my license to live. My family and I enjoyed a good life because others who tried to combine the ingredients all died. That made me indispensable to Hickler. She hated that only one person could make the lethal mixture."

Chasey followed Kessler to the freezer, surprised that it opened without requiring another code. Inside, he identified the containers marked with a triple X as pointed out by Kessler. He picked them up and motioned for Kessler and Donna to head to the door.

They were ten seconds too slow.

An emergency alarm blared throughout the building. Personnel not engaged in dealing with the explosion at the drone factory quickly moved to intercept the intruders.

Tamara and John saw Donna and Kessler exit the factory rapidly, but Chasey was pinned down by automatic rifle fire. John realized Chasey couldn't defend himself while carrying the two marked containers. Slinging his special weapon into action, John sprinted to Chasey's defense. Returning fire, he gave Chasey the space needed to crouch without being hit.

Assessing the situation, John realized the guards would reach the door before he and Chasey could make it to the van. He gave Chasey a friendly shove and pointed to the vehicle. Chasey nodded, running for cover while John stayed behind to hold off the attackers.

Tamara was preparing to leave when the firing abruptly stopped. John sprinted for the van. Donna threw the door open just as John dove inside.

"One submarine place, next stop!" Tamara shouted gleefully.

57

Kim Hickler Poison

Kim Hickler Planning room

Feurth, Argentina

2100 Hours

Reviewing plans for the next stage of the Wolfhead's mission—written decades prior by individuals still revered by many today—Kim Hickler felt honored that the high command had placed their confidence in someone so young. Of course, being a direct descendant of the most powerful authority to ever lead Wolfhead added significant credibility to her position. She had been provided with a security detail of specially trained military personnel, far more advanced than even the highest-ranked "Cleaner."

As she reviewed her plans, she noticed that the latest information from Wilheim had not been entered. *He owes me for allowing him the unique opportunity to take the submarine for his tryst,* she thought. Trusting that Wilheim and his cohorts were capable of discussing the updated status of the worldwide drone armada—still scheduled for deployment within the next four days—she brushed aside the lapse for now.

She tried calling the submarine, but the phone went straight to voicemail. Normally, she would have been incensed at not being able to contact him. Instead, she smiled internally. He and his special unit were currently deploying the poison-laden drones to three separate, densely populated areas—setting the Master Plan of world domination into motion. After Russia, China, and the United States made a vain attempt at recovery, the entire world would bow to Wolfhead's power.

Irritated at not reaching Wilheim, she dialed Braun—only to get his voicemail as well. Now furious, she called Kessler for an update. Again, voicemail—this time punctuated by the unmistakable sounds of nearby explosions.

Peering out her bulletproof window, she saw the drone factory engulfed in flames. There was only one possible explanation. *That damn Hull* must have orchestrated this carnage. Hickler had been well informed of the problems he could cause, based on numerous written and verbal reports brought to her attention.

She depressed the special alarm, alerting her protective force to shift to the highest level of defense. Kim Hickler prided herself on always being able to defend herself. Opening her safe, she extracted the one weapon capable of rapidly bringing death to any living being—human or otherwise.

It looked like a simple, unassuming mahogany-brown walking cane. But it contained the most lethal snake venom known to science. Kessler had analyzed the venom for her, reporting that a human would die less than two minutes after being injected.

A sharp knock on the door was followed by it being blasted off its hinges by a series of powerful strikes from Hull's leg.

"Sorry to ruin your door," Hull shouted. "I wanted one of your staff to properly escort me, but they're all dead—from the same poisonous gas you used to murder thousands. Donna, my doctor and scientific associate, saved several unexploded containers from your latest attack on the United States. She concluded that if a container hadn't ruptured on impact, she could use a few for research. The remainder were placed in an airtight metal container and kept refrigerated by me—until I had a purpose to use them."

He continued, "Your defense strategy failed to consider an attack by poison gas. I threw your own poison gas through an open window while wearing a gas mask for protection. If you look outside, you'll see a few of your men struggling for air."

Hickler assessed her options. Help was unavailable, but Hull's attention was momentarily focused on the dying men outside. She struck him in the calf with her cane.

"You may have temporarily halted our plans," she hissed, "but you will never interfere again. My cane just injected enough venom to kill ten men. I'm surprised you're still standing."

Letting out a loud, raucous laugh that unsettled her, Hull replied, "Your venom would've killed the number you mentioned—but it's been several months since I've felt this good. A snake bit me when I was very young. Doctors at the hospital told my mother there was nothing they could do. She called a shaman friend from the local Indian village who, somehow, saved my life. Since then, I can only use blood taken from my own body if I need a transfusion."

He leaned closer. "Would you mind if I borrowed your cane for another quick jolt? It allows me to sleep just a few hours if needed. The snake blood gives me extraordinary reflexes."

Hull straightened. "You're going to accompany me to your submarine, where a delightful journey awaits you. Turn around—I need to bind your wrists."

For the first time in her life, Kim Hickler realized she was overmatched.

58

Victory Comes with a Cost

Officer; s Quarters

XXI submarine

2200 Hours

Hull handed the handcuffed Hickler to Chasey. "Place her with the others. Kessler and Braun are here—or dead." He didn't wait for a response. He noticed tracks of blood leading to the door.

Jaz recognized Hull's bewilderment. "Gustavo's body is creating quite a stench. Blake and I placed him on the deck of this submarine."

"Splendid idea. Chasey, place Hickler on the front rail of the submarine. Lash her arms and feet to prevent any movement. Do the same to Braun and Kessler—one on each side of her. Leave them ungagged. They deserve a rousing send-off, speaking to each other," directed Hull.

Oddly, none of the others raised an eyebrow at his instructions.

Donna grabbed Hull by the elbow. "We need to speak in private. MadMan and John are in the next room. Unfortunately, it's the only space with sufficient room." She opened the door to the food preparation room. Lying on two adjoining metal tables were MadMan and John. Neither was alert or capable of speaking.

"Hull, I can save MadMan. He suffered a grade four concussion—or worse. He needs cranium and brain scans. Without those tests, any treatment would be a guess. John has stomach wounds which are inoperable. Binding his wounds and sedating him will only delay his passing," Donna said with the experience of someone who had treated such serious injuries before.

Wasting little time, Hull took out his ever-present satellite phone, punching in a series of numbers he had committed to memory. "Two hours before he can be airlifted? That's not good enough, Ashley. What if we were in open water?" Hull was calculating multiple options simultaneously.

Tamara burst into the room. "Roy, there are armed military searching for us. Peters spotted them when she checked on the prisoners."

"That changes my thinking. Pass the word—we are sailing in fifteen minutes. I need to speak with Ashley about our new problem. You two alert the others to prepare for possible enemy action." Hull picked up his phone to speak with Ashley.

John Tsia stood upright from his resting place, wounds showing traces of blood leaking through Donna's bandages.

"Hull, you may prove to be a Superman, but I have piloted Chinese submarines similar to this one while training. Have someone place me in the control room. Dying a lingering death, as Donna described, is not an option for me. I desire a warrior's death." John fumbled, searching for something in his jacket pocket. He pulled out a small box. Carefully, he unwrapped the SPECIAL WARFARES pin awarded to each SEAL upon passing their rigorous training.

"I did not volunteer for your assignment without knowledge of your skill and courage. My father presented your insignia the day I graduated from our special training. He often mentioned how you risked your life to save him. You go on deck to buy time."

Before Hull accepted the valiant offer, he whispered in John's ear, "I must trust you to carry out my final destination for this submarine. I would not consider you any different if you refuse."

John said nothing. He handed Hull his SEAL insignia. "Tell my father I died a warrior's death. Your plan is acceptable to me. Now, get out of my way. I have a submarine to command."

Hull instructed Blake to help John to the control room, make him as comfortable as possible, give him your spare weapon, and hurry back on deck.

On deck, Chasey apprised him of their situation, which was becoming worse by the second.

"I counted three smaller vessels racing toward us. Some of their rounds are far too close for comfort—I mean really too close. In another five minutes, we'll be overwhelmed with small arms fire. Nothing will prevent them from boarding us—if we're not already dead."

Hull glanced at his watch. "Ashley, your rescue schedule better be accurate, or I won't be able to buy you that 'Stolie' I promised."

Chasey hit the deck as bullets flew overhead.

At that exact moment, a submarine—twice as large as the one Hull was using—rose between Hull and the three attacking boats. As it broke the surface, it displayed an American flag. No sooner had it breached the water than Navy personnel raced to the deck guns. The three boats disappeared in seconds under the fierce, unrelenting firepower from the American submarine.

Hull thought to himself, *Ashley, I'll buy you all the alcohol you can drink for saving us.*

Hull directed Blake to inform John to bring their submarine to a complete halt to facilitate transfer of Hull's unit to the American vessel, as discussed with Ashley. Ten minutes elapsed before a small boat could attach to their submarine. MadMan, Donna, Peters, Tamara, and Blake were the first to be transferred.

Watching them depart, Hull told Jaz and Chasey to wait in place. He had to say goodbye to John.

Walking carefully, he descended into the control room for one last conversation.

"I will deliver your final words to your father. I would take you as a partner in any battle. In fifteen minutes, execute the plan we discussed." Hull shook John's hand. "You will die the warrior's death you wanted."

He returned to the deck.

The rescue boat came just minutes after Hull arrived. Safely on board the American submarine, its commander stood on deck, facing Hull.

"I don't know—or care to know—how you could change my assignment from shadowing Chinese submarines, now frequently patrolling these waters. Arguing with Ashley ended as soon as his boss came on the line. Please tell the President I was only following orders. Your request to stay above water to watch your old submarine's progress is no problem."

Hull and his crew gazed into the darkness, watching the lights of the German submarine.

"Are you sending them to freedom?" Jaz asked, visibly indignant.

The question was answered when the lights of the submarine began to disappear underwater—led downward by Kessler, Braun, and Hickler.

"Rest in hell, you bastards," Peters muttered, her sentiment echoing the thoughts of all the others.

59

Vengeance is Sweet

White House Secure Communications Office

Washington D.C,

0600 Hours

Thanks for the use of your secure line—and the coffee. Weak, but appreciated, Hull remarked to John Ashley. "Willi uncovered secret wire transfers between Parris, Novak, and Ming to Kim Hickler, paying for the murder of innocent victims to persuade their countries to invest billions in ineffective defense systems. The real key was targeting areas where the three could plan to strike."

"Sir, your joint calls to Russia and China are live on channel one. Both video and audio will be subject to a ten-second delay due to distance and atmospheric conditions," the unnamed communications specialist said, then closed and locked the door.

Boris, Hull's friend in Russian Special Forces (Spetsnaz), appeared on the screen first.

"Boris, I was hoping to speak to General Tsia at the same time. I forwarded payments—captured by my computer guru, unnamed to protect his identity—to Novak and a woman named Hickler. Hickler was the architect of murdering your civilians in hopes of huge profits. You should have ample proof for any justice to be exacted."

"Fear not. Justice will be swift and soon—by my hands. With your evidence, I can tell you I've always yearned to dispose of Novak. I take it only I, in this country, have this information?" Boris waited for Hull to nod in agreement. Understanding Hull's response, he signed off. The screen went blank.

Hull glanced at Ashley. "Guessing what happened?"

General Tsia's face appeared on the screen, answering Hull's question. "Hull, sorry for the delay. I've been trying to reach my son for the past three days."

"General, permit me to turn your attention to the secret documents I sent only to you. My computer specialist unearthed payments between your countryman, Boa Ming, and a woman named Hickler. The payments were for killing your citizens—for profit. Use the information at your discretion."

He paused, unsure how to approach the next topic.

"Your son died a warrior's death, General," Hull said, the words difficult for any parent to hear. "His last words—he made me promise I would return the insignia I gave you many years ago. I plan to return it in person. Take my word for it: I would serve with him—and you—anytime, anywhere."

Hull stood motionless.

General Tsia bowed and saluted. He spoke very slowly, deeply saddened by the news of his son's death.

"Can you answer me, as one soldier to another? Do you believe Ming was responsible for my son's death?"

Hull answered, "Yes, I believe he was directly responsible."

General Tsia leaned toward the screen, a hint of a tear in his eyes. "I promise you, on my son's honor—Ming will not see another sunset." He saluted and bowed. The screen went blank.

"Max Parris remains the sole criminal still free. He will not escape justice, no matter where he hides," Hull said, his face flushing with anger at the number of Americans murdered in cold blood by Parris's schemes.

John Ashley couldn't hide his smile. "Remember, I had Willi's information before you. Parris made no secret of shredding live humans at his country estate. I had surveillance placed on him around the clock—with the President's approval. Yesterday, he booked flights on three different airlines, at different times and destinations—even though he owns a private Gulfstream. I went to investigate. I found him destroying documents in the shredder. While he was bent over, I tiptoed around him. He never heard me—

too distracted by the shredding noise. I kicked him into the shredder. I left his home to the sound of his screams."

"Well done, my good friend. Time for the drinks I owe you. I chartered a plane to fly Tamara and me to Minot Air Force Base, where Donna is treating MadMan. Drinking and flying don't mix, which means—we can party tonight."

"Just one more thing we have to discuss before we drink on your dime," Ashley said, stopping Hull. "I don't know the exact timeline. Police reports couldn't determine the time of death for a man named Mischa and three of his bodyguards. The bodyguards had their throats slit ear to ear. Mischa's head—according to the report—was split in half. Your travel plans to Argentina were unknown to me. Police attributed the slaughter to gang retribution."

"Sounds like the work of a crazed killer," Hull told Ashley with a slight grin. "Hope I never meet up with him. My throat's getting drier by the minute."

60

Next "STRONG WOMEN STANDING"

Reagan National Airport

Washington D.C.

1000 Hours

Waiting in a well-adorned lounge reserved for special charter customers, Hull was enjoying the strongest coffee he could find. He had cut his usual three-hour daily workout short, still feeling the effects of partying with Ashley into the early hours of the morning.

His regular cell phone buzzed.

"Hull here."

"Please hold for Carson County Sheriff Mason," the voice on the other end requested.

Hull's entire body and psyche went into overdrive, recalling the blood he had spilled in Carson County.

"Hull, this is your favorite meteorologist—Brandon Mason. I'm currently the duly elected sheriff of Carson County. After someone completely burned our county law enforcement complex to the ground, the town came together and rebuilt a much better facility. In addition, the citizens demanded fair elections. Somehow, they elected me."

Hull laughed out loud, disturbing Tamara.

"If you're calling to question me about the fire, I plead the Fifth. Brandon, you'll make a great sheriff. If you ever need my help, you've got my number."

"Funny—that's exactly why I called. I remember you had a close friend at Minot Air Force Base. Would you contact him on my behalf? My mother and their farmer neighbors are experiencing trouble—something that recently turned violent. Give him my number if he needs more info."

"MadMan is in the hospital being treated for a bad concussion. Tamara and I are on our way to visit him. I'll contact your mother in person," Hull explained. "What's her name?"

"Her name is Tina Mason," he told Hull.